A KILLING IN THE SUN

DILMAN DILA

black letter media

First Published by Black Letter Media (Pty) Ltd 2014

Tel: +27 11 966 8061
Fax: 086 606 1565
www.blackletterm.com
info@blackletterm.com

PO Box 94004
Yeoville, 2143
Johannesburg, South Africa

Design & Layout
Black Letter Media (Pty) Ltd

Cover illustration by Rendani Nemakhavhani

Lights on Water, published in The Short Anthology, 2014
Fragments of Canvas, published in Dark Fire, January 2005
Okello's Honeymoon, published in The Swamp, 2004

ISBN: 978-0-9870198-7-5

Contents

The Leafy Man

Japia and a two year old boy were starving under an orange grove. He could get food in Abedo, just a mile away, but everyone in that town was dead. If he went there, he would see the rotting corpses of people he had grown up with, his neighbors, his friends, his loved ones. But if he did not go he would watch the child die of hunger. They hadn't eaten in two days. Now the boy was too weak to cry. Japia did not know his name.

They had enough water. A red brick house with a green iron-sheet roof stood at the edge of the orchard. It belonged to a wealthy farmer, Opata, so did the acre of oranges they were hiding in. His family had fled the morning Miss Doe attacked, not knowing that the best place to hide was right in their backyard. Japia had found food in their kitchen, but now it had run out. They would not be lacking water anytime soon, though, for the house had a rainwater catchment system with a ten thousand liter tank.

He wondered if Opata's family had made it to safety. They had a new van, and the roads were smooth enough for them to speed away. He dreamt about his own family every night. He did not know if they escaped the bloodbath. He did not want to find out. He feared if he did, and it turned out to be a horror, he would lose the little strength he had to survive. It was better to imagine that they had escaped.

He had to go to Abedo.

He put the boy in a kasero, a large basket used for keeping chicken, and secured the lid to ensure the boy does not crawl out. He then shoved the basket into the makeshift hut he had built in the grove, using plywood and grass. It did not bother him that he was caging a child like an animal. He had stayed with the boy every minute since they took refuge in the orchard, watching him, making sure he did not crawl out. Now that he had to ride to Abedo, a cage was the only way to ensure the child did not wander away from the grove. The scent of oranges protected them from Miss Doe.

He cloaked his body, head to toe, in orange leaves. He piled a lot more leaves onto his bicycle. When he stepped out of the grove he looked like a moving shrub. Opata's house was a little over a hundred meters away. It was black, for Miss Doe sat on every inch of the walls and on the roof. Unlike her natural predecessor the anopheles, which had a sight limited to about ten feet, Miss Doe had the eyes of an eagle. She could spot prey a mile away. The moment he emerged from the orchard, she saw him. At once, the cloud rose, like a veil being lifted off the house, revealing the bright green roof, the bright red brick walls, the bright yellow window frames. She floated in small clouds above the rooftop like whiffs of black smoke, and waited for him. She could not attack for the aroma of oranges repelled her.

He paddled his bicycle to the house. The clouds thickened above the rooftop, as more insects flew in to join the wait. Japia's legs felt like a sponge. He felt hollow inside. Every time he ventured out of the grove, he feared Miss Doe would mutate again, that she would learn to tolerate the smell of oranges, and then she would drain his blood.

Not today. The citrus magic still worked.

At the house, the buzzing was so loud that he could not hear anything else. He went to the bathroom. The bugs were so thick on the window that they blocked out the light. He flicked on a torch and stood at the sink for a long moment, looking at the mirror. Shades of gray had blossomed in his hair, which had not tasted a comb in a month. It had become knotty as dreadlocks started germinating on his head. Wrinkles had taken root on his face, making him look twenty years older than forty. He wondered if he was the last man left on earth.

He soaked a cloth in soapy water and wrapped it around his nose. He expected to find a lot of bodies in Abedo town. The stench would be horrible. He did not want to disrespect the dead by spitting, or throwing up. He hoped the wet cloth would be a helpful gas mask.

When he stepped out of the house, he looked toward the orchard. It was a fuzzy blur, for Miss Doe hovered around him creating a thin curtain. An urge to go back to the safety of the grove gripped him, but there he would have to face the eyes of the starving child. He took a deep breath, climbed on the bicycle, and rode to Abedo.

Miss Doe flew all around, at a radius of about ten meters, encasing him in a cylinder as it looked for a chink in his shield. He felt as though he was in the eye of a dust devil. He could not see anything beyond the black wall of the cylinder.

If it were not for her seething, he would have heard the music the tires made as they rolled over the sand. He would have heard the wind blowing, the leaves singing, maybe a pigeon cooing to her lover and children making a racket as they kicked a ball. He would have heard all these sounds a month ago. Now, the only thing in his ears was this buzz. It sounded like rapids raging over the Nile. The hum opened his pores and sweat drenched him.

He rode faster. The bugs kept pace.

#

The government issued him this bicycle three years ago. They had decided to embrace traditional healers and include them in their health strategies, so they launched the Roll Back Malaria Campaign. Government did not recognize herbalists as proper doctors and scientists, but Japia was on a mission to change that attitude. He had served the village as a healer for nearly thirty years, from the age of ten when he inherited the healing spirits after his father died. He had dropped out of formal school, and acquired knowledge the ancient way. He became an expert in plants and diseases and he was a gifted shaman. But to the dismay of the community, he disassociated herbal medicine from spirit worship. He believed mixing the two had hindered the proper research and development of native medical science. Eventually, when they saw him performing greater miracles outside the shrine, they accepted him as a medic only. The government gave him the bicycle to promote insecticide treated nets, but he added his own agenda to the campaign. He knew of plants that repelled mosquitoes with their smell. He promoted growing these plants near homesteads to combat the disease, on addition to simple control methods like cutting bushes, draining stagnant water, and rubbing orange peelings on the skin as a repellent.

The campaign was slowly yielding fruits, with the whole village collectively involved in fighting the epidemic. Then, a company calling itself Pest and Germ Control Corporation came up with a new method. It had modified the genes of the anopheles and created a new species that does not carry malaria parasites. It called this breed, Miss Doe. PGCC asked the government for a trial site. A powerful politician influenced the Ministry of Health to choose Abedo. He thought the project would bring employment to his people, and thus increase his popularity. The genetic scientists from PGCC then camped in the area, and introduced Miss Doe. Their plan was to out-populate and replace the natural mosquitoes with the disease free bugs. A simple plan. A great plan.

Only that, Miss Doe ran riot.

She needed only a day to mature from egg to adult. Within a week, there were thousands. The village woke up one morning to find a lot of dead birds in the grass. Their blood drained. Japia at once suspected Miss Doe. When two cows were found dead later that day also with their blood drained, it confirmed his suspicion. He and other village leaders approached the PGCC scientists, who dismissed the fears. Mosquitoes do not feed on blood, they said, only the females need it for laying eggs. They had fixed that need in Miss Doe. She had no need for blood. The next day, a child was found dead in her bed. A million holes in her skin and not a drop of blood left in her veins. Panic gripped Abedo. Some people fled to neighboring towns. Japia resisted flight. He had discovered that Miss Doe dreaded orange leaves. He placed these on his windows to protect his children. Besides, he thought the worst was over. PGCC publicly acknowledged its mistake and sprayed insecticide over the village to wipe out Miss Doe.

Instead, the chemical triggered off a mutation. Overnight, Miss Doe ballooned from the size of a normal mosquito into a monster as big as Japia's thumb. She no longer looked for food as an individual, but in swarms that swept over the village like dark clouds. Japia had just left home early that morning, to tell his neighbors to use fresh orange leaves as a repellent, when he saw a dark cloud floating over the trees. He heard the screams. He saw people fleeing in terror as clouds of insects chased them. He saw a cloud swallowing up a woman. She fell. Her screaming stopped before she hit the ground. The insects settled on her for only a few seconds, and then rose into the air, leaving her stiff on the ground.

Japia had been too far to go back home to his family, but luckily close to Opata's orchard. He sped to it. On the way, he found the little boy abandoned on the roadside, covered in a blanket.

#

The first corpse he saw nearly made him fall off the bike. The wet cloth around his nose cut out the smell, and his vision was limited to only about ten meters, where the mosquitoes formed an opaque cylindrical wall. He did not see the body until he nearly ran over it. He gripped the brakes. Tires screeched on the sand. The dead man lay partially hidden in the bush, nothing left of him but skin and bones. He knew the coat, gray coat with black stripes. It belonged to the geography teacher, Mr. Okello. Japia used to play scrabble with him every Friday evening, when they would gather in the town square to drink malwa and eat roasted pork. Now Mr. Okello's face stared at Japia with eyeless sockets, with teeth in a lipless mouth that seemed to snarl at him. Flies danced on the body, but he could not hear their buzz. All he heard was the seething of Miss Doe.

He was at the top of a gentle hill. The town lay below. He could not see it through the thin black wall of mosquitoes, but he knew what it looked like. About forty small buildings with red brick walls and corrugated iron-sheet roofs stood in a perfect square enclosing a giant mvule tree. A market thrived in the square. Every Friday, traders travelled from distant districts to sell and thousands of people came to shop, or simply to make merry. The attack had happened on a Wednesday, a quiet day in Abedo, when all the shoppers and traders were locals. All the corpses he would find would be of people he knew. He clenched his teeth, bracing himself, and let the bicycle roll down the sandy road.

Miss Doe kept pace around him, whirring, humming a song of death, stalking him, looking for a chink in his shield, waiting for a chance. He probably was the only moving thing she had seen all month.

He wondered if she could starve to death. Was blood the only thing Miss Doe, fed on? If she killed off every living thing in the area, would she starve?

Japia knew she could not migrate in search of food. Her creators, to protect the technology and ensure maximum profits, fixed her genes so that she could not travel beyond a certain radius from the breeding site where the first egg of the generation hatched. This way, PGCC could charge governments per square inch of land that they had freed of malaria carrying mosquitoes. But how far from Abedo could Miss Doe travel? If Japia was to make a run for it, how far would he get before the orange leaves shriveled and lost the scent that repelled the bloodsuckers?

He rolled into town, between two buildings with roofs arched over the road to form a gate. There were dead people in the square. Fortunately, he could not see the entire market for the murderer's veil obscured his view. A woman sprawled on what once was a pile of fish, maggots crawled in a feast. He recognized her clothing. Mama Samaki, they had all called her. The oldest fishmonger in town. Mama Godi lay in what must have been heaps of potatoes. Two youths, Obore and Kamau, lay on a verandah beside a scrabble game, the last moves still on the board, the book in which they had recorded the scores stuck under a stone. Obore still had a tile in his fingers. Japia had taught them the game just a few months ago. The attack had been so sudden nobody had a chance to flee. Maybe the tree had blocked them from seeing the attackers. Miss Doe needed only a few seconds to drain their blood.

Shop doors were still open. He passed two, with corpses sprawled across the threshold. He recognized Masasa, Kemigisha, Oketch, Ntare. They lay rotting. Japia retched. The wet cloth on his nose was an effective gas mask but his brain conjured up a terrible odor. He tried not to spit, not to vomit, out of respect of the dead. He did not see a corpse in Natasha's shop. It had grains, flour, and nuts, the dry foods he needed. He went in.

A portable radio sat on a shelf, with a copper wire attached to the aerial for better reception. He jumped to it. His fingers trembled as he turned the dial. The batteries were dead. He ripped open a new packet and inserted a pair into the radio, then he tried again. At first, he only got static. He turned the dial until he heard music, the sweet voice of Juliana crooning Nabikowa. The signal was fuzzy, overshadowed by the angry seething of the vampires at the door. He searched for a station with news, but the only one he could pick up was this one playing music.

That in itself was good news. People were still alive out there. They could afford to listen to Juliana. PGCC hadn't lied then; their creation could not travel far from its original breeding zone. *But how far was that?* Japia still wondered.

He hung the radio around his neck with a rope, so he could listen to it as he worked. He packed maize flour, pounded groundnuts, a carton of milk, a bag of sugar, and a box of batteries. He would have to make several trips to carry more food, but this would be enough to feed them for a few weeks. He was looking around for what else he could take when a voice interrupted the music.

He listened. Fuzzy. The radio was picking up two stations. He touched the dial and then he got only the voice station, clear and crisp. Two people were talking in foreign accents. It did not sound like the conversations he used to hear on air. When one spoke there was no background noise, but the other had to shout above a steady roar, like that of a milling machine.

"There's a bit of wind," the one in the noisy place said. "H4 won't spread."

"It will," the other voice said. "Target is two miles away."

"Roger that."

Wazungu. He had interacted with them on many occasions and could understand them, unlike many in Abedo who had found it difficult to pick up their language. As he wondered about the conversation, a sound grew louder outside. It cut through the seething of the mosquitoes, becoming louder every second, until he thought he could recognize it.

A helicopter?

Was he hallucinating?

He dashed out of the shop, scattering the curtain of mosquitoes, and bounded into the square. He searched the skies, but the giant mvule tree blocked his view. He ran out of the market, he ran until there was no tree to block his view, and then he saw it, a white thing shining in the sky. Coming toward him.

It was visible for only a few seconds. Miss Doe closed in around him and blocked his view. He ran again, trying to clear the air of the vampire, and he waved. Frantic. Miss Doe danced around him with increasing frenzy, but he noticed that the wall was thinning. She had also seen the helicopter, and was converging on it.

"There's a black cloud just outside the town," the radio said. Japia recognized the background noise as the roar of the helicopter.

"It's him," the other voice said. "He's waving at you."

A rescue. The tragedy that had befallen his village must have captured news headlines worldwide. They must have been monitoring the area using satellites, or maybe using drones, and they must have seen him riding into town to get food. But how would this helicopter rescue him with Miss Doe gathering around the machine?

The helicopter now flew in circles, spewing a thick white smoke. At first Japia feared it was in trouble, that maybe the mosquitoes had gotten into the engine and caused it to malfunction. His only hope was about to crash. However, unlike normal smoke, the fume did not rise into the air. It fell to the ground like a solid object, and rolled over the grass like a cloud. It provoked tears out of his eyes, but the wet cloth on his nose prevented him from breathing it in.

Almost at once, the buzz of Miss Doe relented. Japia thought the smoke was insecticide, until he saw Miss Doe shooting to the sky in pillars, and then gathering to form a huge cloud that wiped out the sky. It was only a repellent.

"What's happening?" the radio crackled. "We lost the video."

"Where is the drone?"

"The bugs have blocked our view. We can't see anything."

"They cleared the area. We are going down."

"Roger that. Be quick."

The chopper touched down. He could barely see it through the smoke. The engine shut down. The buzz of Miss Doe was faint, but still eerie coming from the sky.

As he started toward the helicopter, four men came running out of the mist. They wore protective white clothing that covered every inch of their bodies. Each had a small tank on the back, and a spray muzzle in one hand. Emblazoned on their breasts were four letters, in bright green, PGCC. Japia's legs turned to water. These men worked for PGCC, the people who brought this apocalypse to his village. It was not a rescue.

He turned and fled.

"Hey!" one man shouted. "Don't run!"

"What's that?" the radio said.

"The leafy man ran," Japia heard the reply coming out of the radio, and from behind him.

"He what?"

"He ran,"

"Why?"

"I don't know. He just saw us and ran."

Japia was weak from hunger, but he was faster that the four men, who were burdened by the heavy tanks on their backs. He knew it was foolish to run. They probably meant him no harm, they might have come to rescue him, but he could not trust them. Not after what they had done to his village. When he was a little boy, his father had campaigned against birth control pills. 'It makes our women barren,' his father had said. 'It's a trick of the white man to wipe out the black man.' Japia had dismissed his father's argument as ridiculous, but with Miss Doe blanketing the sky, he could again hear the old man's warning, and he used all the strength left in his body to run. Stumbling, falling, the chemical stinging his eyes, nearly blinding him. He ran back to the square, to his bicycle.

"Come back!" the men were shouting at him. "We won't hurt you! We came to rescue you! Don't run!"

A strong wind rose. The smoke started to clear. Japia now saw the walls of the town, about eighty meters away. He heard Miss Doe stirring, the irritating buzz that in the past had given him sleepless nights and at worst a bout of malaria, but now amplified a billion times, humming a song from hell.

"Oh fuck," one man shouted. "The bugs are descending."

"Spray more H4," the radio said.

Japia noticed that his oranges leaves had slightly shriveled. Had the chemical killed his shield? He did not want to find out. The mosquitoes were coming back. Fifty meters to the market. A few more seconds of flight, if his strength could hold, but Miss Doe needed only a few seconds to kill.

"Stop!" a man behind him shouted. His voice came from further away. The distance between them was increasing.

"We have to go back to the chopper," the radio crackled. "The wind is too strong for H4 to stay on the ground."

"Don't leave without the leafy man!" Japia took this voice to be that of the man commanding the mission, from a safe place far away.

The breeze turned into a gale. The mist thinned very fast.

"Fuck!"

A black cloud appeared in front of Japia. It flew out of the town and zoomed straight for him. Japia froze. He looked at the shriveled orange leaves, wondering how much power they still had, if they could still protect him. The cloud stopped about ten feet away from him, a lot closer than before. The orange shield had weakened.

He heard a hiss. A jet of white smoke shot past him, and hit the cloud. The mosquitoes broke up, and scattered, and fell to the ground, rolling about in a daze, but not dying, and not fleeing away. They jumped back up into the air, and regrouped into a cloud, painting a huge black spot in the white smoke.

"What the fuck!" the voice came from both the radio and the real world.

"What's happening?" the commander said.

"H4 isn't chasing them off!"

"Nonsense," the commander said. "H4 works. Get the leafy man."

A man screamed. Japia turned to see Miss Doe descending like rain, falling into the white mist, no longer deterred. She had already overcome her fear of the chemical repellent. A cloud fell upon one man, who crumbled to the ground as if under the weight of the cloud. Screaming. The man vanished in the mist. The other men sprayed him with the chemical, but black clouds were swooping down on them as well. One abandoned the cause, and ran, trailing a thick cloud, which overtook him. He fell, screaming.

"What the fuck is going on down there?" the voice in the radio screamed.

The helicopter jumped into the air. Miss Doe gathered around it, enveloping it in a cocoon. The down draught from the propellers could not drive her away. The chopper released more H4. The cocoon broke up, the insects flew about. For a few seconds Japia could again see the chopper, through the black veil. Miss Doe soared above the propellers.

Something bit Japia on the shoulder. It felt like a knife had stabbed him. His shoulder was exposed, without the protection of the leaves. A fat mosquito sat on it, drinking his blood. He slapped at his shoulder. Blood exploded. The mosquitoes were now so close that he could feel the wind from their wings on his face. The shield was weakening. Only a few seconds now and he would be dead.

Not if he reached his bicycle.

He had fresh leaves on the bicycle, unless the chemical had spread into the market and destroyed his only hope.

He ran. A sudden surge of energy boosted him over the tall bushes like an antelope fleeing a lion. A cloud chased him. Another insect drove its proboscis into his shoulder. It felt like a dog had bitten him. He did not slap it away, that would slow him down making him lose precious seconds.

He ran into the market. He flapped his hands wildly, to beat off the insects as they stabbed him in the back, in the face, in the legs. The orange leaves had completely shriveled. The shield had broken down. But he got a fresh boost of energy when he saw that H4 had not touched the square. He ran faster. The bicycle was only ten meters away... the vampires flew after him. He did not stop running until he reached the bicycle. He collapsed at the wheels, and wept.

Screams came from the radio. Voices tumbled out of the speaker like voices whirling inside a madman's head. It reminded him that there was still danger outside. If those PGCC fools sprayed more H4, it would destroy the leaves on his bicycle... Japia threw off the ruined leaves and draped fresh ones on his body.

He rode fast out of town, passed the chopper and the PGCC men battling Miss Doe.

"The bugs are in the chopper!"

"What the fuck," the commander said.

"Echo One. This is Bee. What is happening?" another voice said. Japia had not heard it before. He thought this person was in the command centre somewhere far away.

"The bugs are in the chopper!"

An explosion rocked the world. Japia stopped. He saw flames leaping high into the sky, consuming whole clouds of mosquitoes. Fire can kill her, he thought. The chopper crashed. It was burning. H4 was flammable. The whole area beside the town was burning, the flames consuming more clouds of Miss Doe.

"Holy fuck!" the commander said in the radio. "Fuck! Fuck! Fuck!"

Japia could hear something else above the panic of the voices in the radio, a mighty roar that he mistook for a hailstorm. A dark cloud was spreading above the town. It looked like rain falling in reverse, from the ground toward the sky. Miss Doe was fleeing the flames. She was so thick under the sky that darkness fell upon the world.

#

Japia reached the orange grove a few minutes later. He was afraid that the fire would run out of control and destroy his shelter. It however comforted him that H4 had not spread to a great distance, and that it was the wet season. The vegetation would not burn easily. He crept into his shack and hugged the little boy.

"Do you see him?" the commander said in the radio.

"No sign of him," another voice said. "He could be in any of the little forests."

"We must nuke this place."

"No. She mutates each time we use chemicals. Nukes might not be a good idea."

"Fuck!"

"The leafy man is the key. We must know his secret. We have to find him."

"Fuck! Fuck! Fuck!"

Japia turned off the radio. He would not let them see him again. He would stay hidden, and go to town for more food only in the night. He would work alone to reclaim his village from Miss Doe, for he knew the weapons to use. Oranges, and fire. ✷

The Healer

A whole year had gone and it still hurt him. His hair had turned gray with mourning, though he was barely forty. He sat on a rocking chair, drinking banana wine from a green gourd, his eyes closed. The rain had just stopped. He listened to the music of water dripping off the grass roof. It rhymed with the zephyr rustling through the mango tree. He played an imaginary harp as he composed a tune for his dead wife.

She came to him every night. He recited poems for her, he sang her songs, and he laughed at her jokes. But he could not touch her. They could no longer sit together under the cool mango tree in the heat of the dry season, and listen to parrots calling their names. They could no longer walk hand in hand by the river bank, in open defiance to a world that refused to recognize their marriage.

A rattling erupted.

His eyes flicked open. His nape tickled with the sensation of approaching danger. Wings flapped. A bird sped through the chilly noon. Little Acii. An ajwaka, like him, but one who the ancestors said would lead their people, the Twa, out of slavery. She seemed to be running for her life.

Benge placed the gourd on the table, slipped into a pair of wooden sandals, and hurried out of the door. He stood on the verandah, scanning the sky. Wet leaves sparkled in the cool sun, which peeped like a shy ghost from behind a gray cloud. A lot of birds flew about. He could not tell which one was Acii until a brown parrot landed at his feet, and materialized into a twelve year old girl. She was a little too tall for her age. Her hair was plaited into four neat rows of hills.

"They are coming!" she said, breathless.

He opened his inner ears, and heard the robot horses charging on the road. They were still three miles away. They had been hunting him from the day his wife had died. They wanted to re-enslave him and take the six square miles of land that she had left him.

"Somebody kidnapped a child," Acii said. "They think it's you."

"A child?"

"Yes. Raluf."

Benge remembered, Raluf, a slightly overweight boy who had tasted death after a snake bite. The Oksian priest and Cuku doctors, in spite of great advancements in science, had no solution for the venom. They could only watch as the boy's life slipped away. His mother had secretly brought him to Benge, and then the boy had survived. The miracle had softened the hearts of a few more Cuku towards Benge. Some talked about converting him to Oksism, so that he could use his magic in line with their religion. Without the support of these liberals, who sneaked him supplies in the night, Benge would not have survived this long. If it weren't for these liberals, he might have been convinced to become an Oksian so he would not have to live in hiding and to appease the conservatives. But they wanted him to serve in the temple as a slave. He could not agree to that.

The Cuku and the Twa had been enemies for centuries. The Cuku had skin the color of ripe bananas, and bright red hair that grew straight and stiff like grass. They believed Oks had created the world and given them dominion over all living things. They saw themselves as superior to the Twa, whose skin was the color of roasted coffee and whose hair grew thick like sheep wool. In the past, a great, impenetrable desert had separated the two nations. Then the Cuku invented flying ships, crossed the desert, conquered the Twa and enslaved them. After four centuries, some Cuku had started to protest against slavery. His late wife, Lachila, had gone a step further to free all her slaves, and even marry one. But the moment she had died, the conservatives put them back in chains. Only Benge remained free. He used juju to hide himself and his home. The Cuku never stopped hunting for him. He could hear them screaming for his blood as their metallic horses charged towards his land.

"I can strike them," Acii said. Her eyes turned reddish, resembling that of an eagle, as she summoned storm clouds. Lightning was her favorite weapon.

"Stop it," he said.

She was the slave of an old couple. They were cruel to her. Ever since the jok possessed her, and transformed her into an ajwaka, three months ago, she craved for revenge. Benge struggled to restrain her, to teach her that revenge was evil. She had to keep her powers a secret until the time was right for her to lead the Twa out of slavery.

"Why do they think I took him?" he said.

Her eyes changed back to normal, but the storm clouds stayed in the sky, prowling about like eager soldiers waiting to defend their master.

"A juju carriage took him," she said.

It had happened a little over an hour ago. A black substance had covered the sun, plunging the day into night, like an eclipse. Benge had not seen the darkness, though his home was only a few miles from the town. Six horses, real flesh and blood horses, had charged out of a dust devil, dragging a carriage, a green box with gold-framed doors and windows. It had no driver. A panel on the sunroof opened, a noosed rope flew out and snared the little boy. It sucked him into the carriage, which vanished into another pillar of dust.

Benge could understand why they suspected him. The few liberal Cuku who consulted him traveled to his home in a juju carriage, which he provided. That way, they were never able to figure out the exact location of his home, though they knew it was somewhere within the six square miles that his late wife had left him.

"Let's go to town," Benge said.

"But they are coming," Acii said. "They'll burn your house."

He smiled. He started to sing, as he faced the house. He had built it as a grand Twa palace. It was round, with ten rooms and a grass roof. Clay and ash gave the mud walls a red and white color. The windows and doors were blue, fashioned out of papyrus reeds. As he sang, the house vanished. A bush sprang up, wiping out the pathway, and all signs of habitation.

"You didn't teach me that!" Acii said, sucking her teeth.

"Meet me in town," Benge said. "Stay out of sight."

"You hide from them like a coward," she said, sprang into the air, turned into a parrot, and flew away.

She favored an all out war with the Cuku. Benge was against it. Though it could lead to victory, it would do nothing to convince the Twa to return home. Many had become ardent followers of Oks. They interpreted many verses in the holy book to mean that they, not the Cuku, were the true children of Oks. They relished their status as slaves because of one verse; '*And Oks shall bring his lost children back in airships, and they shall be sold as slaves for disobeying him and wandering away from home.*' They believed if they obeyed their masters, they would live forever in paradise. Benge knew Cuku priests had added that verse four hundred years ago to subjugate the Twa. The jok had showed him all these things. But many Twa believed in Oks and considered ajwaka, like him and Acii, to be evil. They had murdered their own children who had become possessed with the jok. Before they could defeat the Cuku in war, they had to first decolonize the minds of the Twa.

Benge closed his eyes, chanted a spell, and teleported himself to a wet, gray road. It ran from the town and passed by his land. In earlier attempts, the Cuku had charged into his property and scoured every bush, but he had temporarily blinded them with juju. They could see, but not understand what they were seeing. He made them roam about in circles until they found themselves back in town. They had then tried to set his land on fire, but he summoned a big storm to put out the flames. They knew the hunt was futile, yet they never stopped trying to find him. He could now hear their robot horses with his corporeal ears. The hoof beats grew steadily louder as they charged up a steep slope on the other side of the hill. Soon, a head appeared at the top of the road. It wore a black hat with a red sun painted on it. The mayor.

When the mayor saw Benge, his robot horse stopped so suddenly that sparks flew off its hooves. Its silver body gleamed in the sun. Its eyes glowed green like emeralds. An engine whirred inside its belly. The mayor was a liberal. He secretly visited Benge in the wee hours of the night to talk to his dead wife. But now Benge could see disappointment in his eyes. His face clouded in anger. He pulled an arrow gun out of his hip holster.

Benge threw his hands up in surrender. "I didn't do it," he said.

The mayor's gun beeped as he switched it on. A red light blinked just below the barrel, and a red dot appeared on Benge's forehead.

"Where's he?" the mayor asked.

A parrot squawked. It was perched on a wire pole. Acii. The storm clouds hung low. Thunder crackled. A breeze rose. When she was in a transformed state, he could not speak to her. He hoped she would refrain from doing something that would give away her secret.

"I didn't take him," Benge said.

The other Cuku came over the hill. There were twenty of them. On seeing Benge, they stopped behind the mayor. They aimed their arrow guns at Benge.

A priest appeared last. His horse stopped beside the mayor. He wore a black flowing robe and had pinned a tongi on his chest. It was a powerful Oksian symbol of a heart and four arrowheads.

"Kill him," the priest said.

Lightening struck a nearby tree, setting it on fire. The thunder that followed deafened Benge for several seconds. Several men fell off their horses, clutching their ears in pain. Benge cast a warning glance at the parrot. Acii wriggled her tail as though to say it was just as a warning.

"I can help you find him," Benge said to the mayor.

"Just tell us where he is," the mayor said. His finger trembled over the trigger button. Sweat dripped off his chin.

"I don't know where he is," Benge said. "But I can help find him."

"Kill him!" the priest screamed.

"No!" the mayor shouted.

He switched off his gun, and turned his horse around to face the other Cuku. They were recovering from the freak thunder, picking up their guns and remounting their horses. One or two were still deafened.

"We failed to find his house before," the mayor continued. "If we kill him, we might never find the boy."

The priest's eyes turned as red as his hair. "Are you disobeying Oks?" He spoke in a voice that reminded Benge of a cat's purr. "Are you siding with the evil Wiir?"

"No," the mayor said. "But we need his cooperation to find the boy."

The priest now ignored the mayor. His authority surpassed that of the elected official. He had all along led the hunt for Benge, and now that Benge was in his sight, he could not let the chance go. He turned to the men.

"Kill him," he said.

Several men squeezed the trigger buttons. The guns made low popping sounds as finger-length arrows shot out. Benge muttered a protection spell. He did not flinch as the arrows whizzed past his ears. The men glanced at their weapons in confusion, unable to believe how such a sophisticated technology could miss the target. Each gun had a miniature screen at the top. The men tapped Benge's image on the screen, identifying him as the target, and fired again. This time, the arrows gathered an inch in front of Benge's face. He suspended them in the air for several moments, and then let them drop.

Another bolt of lightning struck the burning tree. The men pressed their fingers into their ears, but when the thunder came, the sound knocked them all off their horses. Benge remained standing. He glared at the parrot. Acii wriggled her tail again.

The Cuku scrambled to their feet, and staggered about in a daze, clutching their ears in agony. The priest touched his tongi and broke into loud prayers, asking Oks to strike the witch dead, but Oks did not exist.

Thousands of years ago, a king, wary of the power of magicians, had created this god and banished magic from his kingdom. He decreed that everyone should worship only Oks. Over the years his religion had become popular. The book he wrote became holy, and was believed to contain the absolute truths of life.

As the priest prayed, the mayor staggered to Benge.

"We need your help," his voice croaked as though he had not tasted water in a year. "But I have to make you a prisoner. Please, understand. It's the only way we can work together."

Benge nodded in agreement.

#

Benge rode in a prisoner's cage attached to the mayor's horse. The twenty gunmen and the priest rode behind him. The landscape changed drastically from a lush green to a desolate wasteland as they neared Chokon town. Oksism philosophy told the Cuku that this world was a temporal home, that it was the kingdom of the evil Wiir and that their real home was a paradise somewhere beyond the stars. Having abandoned magic, they adopted destructive technologies to run their lives; cutting down trees, building factories that spewed poison into the air, making machines that filled the water with filth. The river just outside the town had become a sewage canal. They burrowed into the earth looking for mineral fuel for their robot horses and flying ships, leaving a wake of destruction. They did not care that the amount of rainfall was dropping, the droughts lengthening, the crop yields getting poorer, or that the desert was creeping upon them. After all, Oks would soon take them to paradise.

Benge and his captors entered the town. The brightly colored box shaped buildings gave Chokon a rainbow façade. A bright green temple stood in the middle, towering over all the other buildings. It had twelve spires, each with a clock ticking an incessant hymn. A pillar soared in front of the temple. It held up high a giant tongi, making it visible for miles all around. The courthouse, with a scale of justice on the roof, stood opposite the temple.

It might have been a beautiful town, but piles of cables ran over the streets, snaking off poles and into buildings in messy crisscrosses. The excrement of marabou storks smeared the walls. Hundreds of the birds, attracted by the garbage, graced the rooftops, along with a multitude of tall disc-shaped aerials that tapped communication signals from the city five hundred miles away.

Faces peered out of the round windows, people crowded the oval doors, small groups stood on the dusty pavements, watching the mayor drag in the witch. Nobody dared go into the road, where the ghost carriage had left tracks on the stones. The mayor stopped on reaching the tracks. He climbed down from his horse and opened the cage, letting Benge out. The priest and the twenty men stopped too, their guns drawn.

Benge knelt beside the tracks. Someone threw a stone at him. It bounced off his shield without harming him.

"Stop it!" the mayor said.

"He's a witch!" someone screamed. "Why do you bring him into our holy town?"

Benge did not pay any attention to the shouting. He touched the track. A psychic flash of light hit him.

He saw a green carriage, a noosed rope taking a boy, a different boy who was a little younger than Raluf. Benge knew him too. Acii's mother was a slave in the boy's house. The carriage vanished into a plume of dust, and materialized in a diary farm. He recognized it from the aerogenerator with blue blades.

"Nurda's farm," he said to the mayor. "Take me there."

"What?" the mayor said, barely audible for his voice had dropped to a shocked whisper. "Nurda's farm?"

"We have to search it," Benge said.

He had not had a vision of the past, but of the future. The carriage would come again to take another boy. But why?

"Are you sure?" the mayor said, still whispering in disbelief. "Nurda is –" he broke off. Benge knew what he wanted to say. Nurda was a cousin to the priest. Their family had founded the town over a hundred years back. It had become a tradition for their clan to fill the most important positions in the temple.

All along, Benge had assumed a fellow Twa ajwaka had taken the boy. There were about a dozen scattered all over the Cuku Empire. They did not practice evil magic. They used their powers only for good, with utmost restraint and secrecy. But one of them might have turned rogue and kidnapped the boy. It had been a viable theory until now.

A Cuku practicing magic was unheard of. They were all Oksians. A few, like the mayor, consulted Twa ajwakas in secret, but they were incapable of practicing magic. Now, Benge had to entertain the idea of a Cuku sorcerer, however farfetched it seemed. There was no way a Twa could practice magic in a place so close to Benge's home without Benge knowing about it.

"Okay," the mayor said. "Let's go."

Benge took a step toward the cage, but the priest's horse blocked his way.

"Where are you going?" the priest asked.

He had let the mayor bring Benge into town because he thought they were going to torture Benge into revealing the location of his house and the boy, and then lynch him.

"He knows where the boy is," the mayor said.

"Is he confessing?" the priest said.

The mayor turned to Benge. "Are you confessing?" he asked.

Benge did not answer. He did not have to subject himself to humiliation. He could teleport himself out of the town if he wanted to, but he had a plan. It was time to shake the people's faith in Oks, and begin the campaign to win the minds of the Twa.

"Put me in jail," he said to the mayor. "You go search that place."

"Not jail," the priest said. "The pillar."

A grate sat at the base of the pillar that towered in front of the temple. On this grate they burnt offerings to Oks, and they destroyed with fire all things they believed to be evil.

"Don't worry about me," Benge said to the mayor. "You go find that boy."

They strapped Benge to the pillar. The grate was cold and wet. He squinted as the sun shone into his face. He searched the crowd for Acii, but did not see her. When a cloud quickly swept across the sun, throwing a shade upon the town, he knew she was nearby, watching him. She had to be one of the marabou storks on the rooftops, still a child, still his apprentice, but for the moment his protector.

He could not do anything about the dust. It rose every time a breeze blew, clogging his nose and mouth. Sweat stuck to his back. He felt as though a sticky porridge had drenched him. He hated the odor, which wafted from the overflowing garbage bins and from the river turned sewage canal.

He recognized some of faces gathered on the temple steps, the Twa slaves and Cuku liberals who sought his help in secret. Uncertainty wavered in their eyes. They wondered if he had kidnapped the boy, if indeed he was evil.

The mayor jumped on his horse, and took ten men with him. He did not tell the priest where he was going, but the priest did not seem eager to find out. They went off in a cloud of dust. The sound of metal hooves echoed long after they had vanished.

Then a silence fell, broken only by the chorus of the twelve ticking clocks. The priest walked into the temple. The spangles on his boots jingled. He returned with a jar of holy oil. The crowd burst into a lynch hymn. They sang for several minutes, and then the priest raised a hand. The singing stopped.

"In the pillar of Oks," he said, "the power of evil shall not prevail."

"Emona!" the crowd roared.

He poured some of the oil into the grate, and the rest of it onto Benge. It was cold and greasy. Lightning flashed, thunder blasted into the town. Acii was warming up to protect Benge. A stork spread its wings towards the sky, standing still, its eyes fixed on him. He gave a slight shake of his head. Don't do it. He could not read the expression on its face. The priest looked up at the sky, a frown of worry knitted on his brows. The memory of the freak thunder showed on his face, interwoven with the knowledge that Oks would not come to his aid.

The crowd degenerated into delirious singing and prayers, calling upon Oks to destroy evil and return Raluf safely home. But some people, his secret visitors, were silent, watching with confusion on their faces.

"I am not evil," Benge whispered. He used magic to ensure

everybody heard him. A sudden hush fell upon the town. "If Oks stands for good, then I am a servant of Oks. I heal the sick. I help the bereaved to find peace. I nurse wounded minds back to sanity. I never kidnap little boys."

"He's charming us!" the priest shouted.

He pressed a button on the igniter in his palm. Fire leapt out of the grate and licked Benge's feet. Flames ran all over his body, but they died out almost at once. He was unhurt. His clothes unburnt. The fire sizzled in the grate, weak and harmless.

The crowd let out a collective gasp of shock and stepped away from the pillar. The priest continuously pressed the igniter button, but the fire stayed in the grate. Shouting the name of Oks, the priest fled into the temple.

"If I were evil," Benge continued in a soft voice, "then surely Oks would have destroyed me. But look, he saved me."

He had to play on their beliefs. It was too early to tell them that Oks was a fallacy. He had to make them believe he was a servant of Oks. Gradually, he would win the minds of the Twa. They would come to see him, and other ajwakas, as the true servants of Oks, and that Cuku priests merely used Oksism to ensure their subjugation to slavery.

"This pillar bears the power of Oks," he said. "I should be roasted by now, but Oks protected me. He asks me to deliver to you a simple message. You've been deceived for long. The book has been misinterpreted. Today, you'll see the true servant of Oks."

The priest ran out of the temple, this time with a bigger jar of oil, which he poured on Benge. But not a drop fell on the prisoner. The oil splashed onto the stones, and ran into the grate, fanning the flames, which did not harm Benge.

"The book says that Oks forbade making symbols of him,"

Benge continued. He pointed at the tongi on top of the pillar. "Why then do you worship that?"

Acii understood the cue. A bolt of lightning struck the tongi. It exploded, showering the crowd with concrete and dust. People fled from the temple, screaming.

"The book says your body is the temple of Oks," Benge said, again projecting his voice above the clamor. "Why then do you treat this building as the temple?"

A second bolt of lightning struck the temple, setting its roof on fire. Sirens blared. The priest ran into the building to save his valuables. The crowd fled from the street. Within a few seconds, the street was empty. Benge broke the chains binding him to the pillar and stepped off the grate. The pillar disintegrated into a pile of rubble.

He jumped on the priest's horse, and galloped fast out of the town. A marabou stork flew beside him until they were out of sight. Then it jumped onto the seat behind him, and materialized into Acii.

"Where are you going?" she said.

"To Nurda's farm," he said.

"Why do you use this?" she said. "Teleporting is quicker."

"I don't know what lies there," he said.

They used juju to travel faster than the actual speed of the robot and covered ten miles in about eight minutes. The mayor and his men were waiting at the gate, a giant red metal structure with tongi painted on it.

"I'll stay out of sight," Acii said. She leapt into the air, turning into a parrot. Benge thought it was her favorite bird. She flew ahead of him. He reached the gate just as an old slave swung it open. The mayor was not surprised to see Benge, but his men seemed terrified.

"How did you convince the priest to let you go?" the mayor said.

"I burnt his temple," Benge said.

"You what?"

"The boy is not here," Benge said.

"What?"

Benge galloped to the farm houses, scanning the air for spirits and juju. He found nothing out of the ordinary. Why then had he seen this farm in the vision? There were no horses or carriages in the barn. Hundreds of cows ate factory prepared food in the kraals. Scores of slaves milled about, cleaning the stalls, refilling bowls, milking cows. No sign of Raluf. He went through the slave quarters, the master's cottage, and the visitor's lodge. Nothing. He met the mayor and Nurda in front of the cottage. Nurda's face was tense with anger. He had a gun in each hand.

"The culprit built a vision of this place to make me think the boy is here," Benge said. "It's an old trick and I fell for it."

"So where is the boy?" the mayor asked.

"I don't know," Benge said. "I need fresh clues."

#

Benge and the mayor waited until midnight, when the town was asleep and the streets empty, before continuing their investigations. The full moon sat just above the burnt temple roof, bathing one half of the street with light while the other sat in a shadow. The spangles in the mayor's boots jingled as they walked down the road. Other than this, the night was silent. All the twelve clocks were damaged. For once their incessant song did not grace the town.

Benge could not find another clue.

"It will return," he said. "It will take another boy. Chalina's son."

"When?" the mayor asked.

"I think tomorrow."

"Should we send him out of town?" the mayor said.

"No," Benge said. "Keep all the children indoors. Let's prepare for a fight."

#

Overnight, the division in the town surfaced. After Benge's public demonstration, the liberals not only marginally grew in number but became bold enough to openly question Oksism. The conservatives interpreted what had happened to be a test of their faith. Wiir has powers, they argued. He rules this world. Sometimes Oks allowed him to prevail to test his followers.

The next morning, the priest accused the mayor of siding with evil. A mob formed in the ruined temple to lynch the mayor. The liberals, however, learnt of the plans to attack the courthouse, and gathered to support the mayor. When the mob started to march from the temple across the street to the courthouse, a barrage of arrows fell at their feet. No one was hurt. These were only warning shots. The conservatives retreated into the temple, and took position on the burnt rooftop, and in the windows. War erupted. Arrows flew across the street.

Benge and Acii were on a rooftop at the far end of the street, waiting for the carriage. They watched the events unfolding in the town with great dismay. The only advantage of the fight was that it left the streets empty, and it stayed that way until the carriage returned at noon.

The black substance appeared in the sky. Within a few seconds, darkness fell upon the town. Benge and Acii could still see the sun behind the clouds, but it was just a pale disc. Screams rang all over. Windows slammed shut as people ducked into hiding. The priest broke into loud prayers.

Acii turned into a stork and soared. Her lightning blazed in the sky, but it could not penetrate the black substance. She summoned a mighty gale. It blew through the town, sweeping away storks and aerials, ripping off a few roofs, but the black substance did not move. As she huffed and puffed, a dust devil formed at the edge of town. It moved fast into the main street, growing larger and taller with each spin. Six horses jumped out, one pair after the other, and last came the carriage. It thumped into the street.

Benge jumped down and stood in the middle of the road. He held out his palms, chanting a spell to freeze the demon. The horses kept charging. A noosed rope darted out of the carriage and crashed into a window. Glass shattered. It vanished into a room, lengthening as it flew out of the carriage. The horses kept running at top speed. Their eyes, fixed on Benge, shone like pearls in the darkness. He conjured an invisible brick wall, but the beasts broke through with ease.

They knocked him aside. The contact sparked a bright flash of light. He fell, every inch of his body on fire as a psychic current unveiled the sorcerer in the carriage. Just as Benge had suspected the previous day, it was a Cuku. Still, the identity of the man behind it all shocked him. Kasito. One of the most holy Oksians he knew.

The horses raced through the town. Benge leapt to his feet, ignoring the pain, and pursued them. The rope came out of the room, a screaming boy tethered to it. His parents leaned out of the window in a desperate attempt to grab their son, but the rope was sucking him into the carriage, far out of their reach.

Acii turned into an eagle. She grabbed the rope with her talons and worried it with her beak. The rope tried to suck them both into the carriage. Benge spat a huge lump of mucus. It landed on the roof, sizzling, smoke spewed as wood burnt. The rope broke. The boy started to fall. Acii swooped down and grabbed him a moment before he smashed his head on the stone road.

Benge spat out another glob of mucus, thicker than before, to trap the carriage and prevent it from leaving, but he was a few seconds too late. The dust devil appeared. A portal opened, and Benge saw a tall red house with round green windows in the middle of a cotton field. The horses jumped in. The portal closed. The dust vanished.

Behind him, Acii fought with the rope. It had become serpentine, and was squeezing the boy, like a python trying to crush prey. She was still an eagle, her talons between the boy's flesh and the rope. The black substance cleared from the sky, allowing her to use lightning. She struck the rope, at a point that might have been the snake's tail, setting it on fire. The rope released the boy. It dropped to the ground and burnt to ash.

Acii took the boy in one claw and flew back up the street. His parents were still leaning out of the window, praying for Oks to spare him. Acii put him in their outstretched hands, and they pulled him into the safety of the room. Then she returned to the rooftop and changed into a little girl.

Benge found her panting in exhaustion, her body bruised from the fight. She bled above her eyes. He touched the wound. The bleeding stopped and the cut slowly vanished.

"Are you ok?" he said.

She nodded. "I just need to catch my breath," she said.

#

Though most of them had stayed hidden and did not see it happen, the second attack convinced many of the conservatives that Benge had nothing to do with Raluf's disappearance. Chalina and his wife, whose son he had saved, spoke of how he fought against the evil carriage. The testimony did not win the Oksians over, but it at least compelled them to listen to Benge.

"It's a Cuku sorcerer," he said. "A man you all know. Kasito."

He stood in the middle of the road, between the temple and the courthouse, with the two factions on their respective sides, still wielding arrow guns.

"Liar," someone said. "We Cuku don't use magic."

"It's you backward slaves who use magic," another person said.

"Kasito is a good Oksian," the priest said.

Kasito was the only Cuku in town who did not own slaves. He used robots to run his farm. He lived alone with three sons. He attended Oksian rituals every week, and was often the largest contributor whenever the priest needed funds to run temple activities.

"You'll find the boy in his basement," Benge said. "They'll turn him into a robot to work the farm for the rest of his life. All of his robots were once people."

A murmur of disbelief rippled through the town.

"The boy is alive because he has a big scar on his back," Benge continued, again projecting his voice above the murmur. "Kasito wanted him for a sacrifice to an ancient power that you know as Wiir. It can only work if he offers a young boy without any scars or missing body parts, that's why he attempted to take another kid today. I could go out there to fight him, but then you'd never believe me. So go see for yourselves."

With that, he walked out of town, leaving them in a thick silence.

He did not go back home. He settled under a mango tree and opened his inner eyes and ears to follow what happened next. The psychic current had told him everything about Kasito, a sorcerer who hated Oksism because it destroyed the world. Forests were vanishing, animals were becoming extinct, the climate was changing at an alarming rate, all because Oksism made people believe this world was not their home. Kasito wanted power to defeat Oksism, to make people see that paradise was the world they lived in, not a mythical place beyond the stars. The dramatic kidnaps were his first shots in the war against Oksism. His cause was noble, but he thirsted for the power of the gods. He wanted the power to make the sun stand still, to wipe out stars and change the shape of the moon. He believed he could achieve it through human sacrifice.

The mayor prevailed upon the town to, at least, search Kasito's house. The two sides then stopped their war, formed a posse and sped to the cotton farm. The priest and the mayor rode beside each other, ahead of forty volunteers. Acii followed the posse as an eagle, watching from amidst the clouds. A robot opened the farm gate. The men sped through miles of cotton to the red house. They found Kasito, his three sons, and Raluf, waiting on the front porch.

"I can't believe this," the priest said.

"Well," Kasito said. "You won't believe that you worship a false god either."

"Oks is not a false god," the priest said.

Kasito smiled. "Look," he said. "Let's not fight. We've been friends all our lives and I don't want to kill anyone. Here is the boy. He is unharmed. Take him away. In the morning, we'll be gone. Me, my sons, and the farm. When you return you'll find nothing but a wilderness. We'll start a new life very far away from here."

"You –" the priest started to say something, maybe to insist on Kasito burning at the grate in front of the temple, but the words could not come out.

"We'll publish your picture in the news," the mayor said. "The whole world will know what you did. Wherever you go, they'll know you are evil. They'll lynch you."

Kasito shrugged. "I can live with that," he said. "Leave now, or else you'll never find your way out."

Without another word, the mayor put the boy on the back of his horse and sped away from the red house. The priest and the men followed. Kasito remained on the porch, watching them go in a cloud of dust. He must have thought there would be no war, for when Acii's lightning came, he had no protection. It struck him in the head, splitting open his skull and searing the flesh off his bones. It took Benge by surprise too.

The three sons watched the sky in resignation but Acii swept away the clouds and called up a rainbow. It was a sign that she was sparing them. They conjured doves to fly around their house in acknowledgment. They knew magic. Benge realized that they could be valuable allies in the campaign against Oksism. He decided to make them his students.

#

Three days later, Benge got a surprise call. The mayor burnt incense in a clay bowl and chanted a phrase, which wafted to Benge like a prayer. He was taking a nap, and woke up with the voice of the mayor in his ears. For a moment he was confused. He could not understand why the mayor was contacting him at day time. He opened his inner eyes, and saw the mayor performing the ritual in the conference room of the courthouse. There were thirty people around the table, including the priest. The town's council. Many were radical conservatives. Was it a trap? Had they forced the mayor to contact him?

He sent a carriage. Unlike Kasito's, his was a simple two-wheel vehicle made of plain wood and drawn by a single horse. It rode up the street in a gentle gallop. Town folk came out to watch as the mayor boarded it. No one shouted insults, or threw missiles at the juju vehicle. The carriage vanished from the street. The people turned away and went on with their businesses.

A few minutes later, Benge sat with the mayor under the mango tree in front of his house, drinking banana wine out of gourds, listening to the zephyr in the tree.

"Kasito's children came to us this morning," the mayor said. "They pleaded for forgiveness. They said they did not know their father practiced magic. They want to stay. The priest is against it. He wants them to leave. But the town council voted in their favor. It was a narrow win, sixteen ayes and fourteen nays. But before we make a final decision, we need your opinion. Are these boys are evil? That's why I came."

Benge smiled. He had visited Kasito's sons the previous day, and offered to mentor them. They had accepted. They had never been comfortable with their father's quest to gain more power using human sacrifice, but they were eager to continue the war he had started against Oksism.

"They are innocent," Benge said. "Don't punish them for sins of their father."

"But they use those juju robots," the mayor said. "You told us they were once people. How can they be innocent? How could they not know?"

"Yes," Benge said. "Those robots are dead people. Zombies. The boys knew. But they were under the influence of their father. They are willing to cooperate. They have agreed to get rid of the robots and employ humans to work the farm."

"Good," the mayor said. "The council will be happy to hear that."

A brief silence settled between the two men.

"Do you want to talk to her?" Benge asked. The mayor had previously visited only to talk to his dead wife.

"No," he said. "Let her rest in peace."

Benge thought about his dead wife, maybe he too should let her rest. With the changes happening in town, he would not have to stay in hiding anymore. He would not be lonely anymore. Maybe it was time for him to find a new wife.

"Yes," he said. "Let her rest in peace." ✷

Itanda Bridge

The soldiers came shortly before sunrise. Obil was brushing his teeth in front of his muzigo. Most of his neighbors were already up, washing clothes, cooking breakfast on charcoal stoves in front of their doors, or cleaning their teeth and spitting into the gutter that ran through the compound. The smell from the drainage channel overpowered the stench of the fish market, in which the compound was situated. The bustle of activity made the narrow courtyard look like a tunnel in an anthill. There were two rows of about thirty doors facing each other, leading to single roomed muzigos. Unlike Obil who lived alone, every other apartment had a family of about four. There were so many children, and they made so much noise that Obil almost did not hear the soldiers approaching.

Vehicles rarely came this early to the market, so when an engine hummed, a sudden hush fell upon the courtyard. It sounded like a truck. Obil's business did not have much competition. He owned a motor canoe, which took passengers to islands. But his neighbors were fishmongers, and the sound of the approaching truck meant an approaching buyer. A few people cursed because they had not woken up early enough, while a man started to blame his wife for making him oversleep. Then, panic gripped the market when someone shouted 'kichwa red!' His neighbors scrambled into their muzigos, locking the doors. Several people fled from the street into the courtyard, and ducked into the row of pit latrines to hide.

Within a few seconds, Obil remained alone in the courtyard. Kichwa red was slang for a commando unit. They wore red caps, and were famous for panda gari, the cordon and search operations to root out terrorists. The people they captured, although innocent, were never seen or heard of again. Obil wanted to run and hide, like his neighbors, but that would be useless. He knew the soldiers had come for him.

He looked around, at the abandoned basins full of soapy water, at a toothbrush with paste still on it, thrown into the gutter, at a baby's shoe with holes in the toes, at the clothes on the wires dripping onto the dirt yard, at the dozens of charcoal stoves, some of which had been upturned in the panic to hide. The smell of burning food now mingled with that of the gutter, and of fish.

The vehicle screeched to a halt, its tires grinding on the tarmac, adding the stench of rubber to the complex odors of the market. Boots thumped through a muddy corridor as the soldiers charged to the compound. The first gunman burst through the small wooden door. His cap was the color of fire. His uniform was plain green. He had a sergeant's stripes, and carried a pistol. Behind him came five soldiers, also in red caps, but whose uniforms had yellow leopard spots.

Obil threw his hands up in surrender. He still had a toothbrush in one, a plastic mug in the other. His lips smeared with foam. He wore nothing but shorts. The sergeant walked up to him, and gave him a reassuring smile. Obil kept his hands high above his head. The sergeant took a photograph out of his pocket, glanced at it, and then put it away.

"Come with us," the sergeant said.

"Let me get dressed," Obil said, wondering where they got his picture.

The soldier did not respond, but he did not do anything when Obil resumed cleaning his mouth. They watched him in silence. He spat into the gutter, and then walked into his muzigo. He had suspected they would come for him from the day they occupied Itanda Bridge, a week ago. A rumor had spread that they were looking for divers. The previous day, when news broke out that three vehicles had crashed off the bridge and plunged into the river, Obil had become certain that they would come for him. He thought they wanted divers to drag bodies out of the water.

Inside his room, he looked at the row of clothes hanging on hooks on the wall. He could not decide what to wear. He thought of his new clothes, a checkered shirt and a pair of blue jeans. He had saved for three months to buy them. He planned to wear them on Christmas day, when he would ask Amito to marry him. It would be tragic if he died before using them. He mulled for a moment, and decided that wearing them might bring bad luck, so he settled for his work clothes, torn jeans and a worn-out t-shirt.

They drove for an hour, out of the small lakeside town, up a slick road, and then onto the highway that connected the city to the coastal port of Mombasa. A line of vehicles, three miles long, was stranded at the roadside. The soldiers had closed the highway after the accident. Tanks blocked the road five miles to the bridge. As they neared Itanda, Obil noticed a drastic change in the vegetation. The trees were dead. The branches bare and black, as though a wild fire had burned them. The grass had a sick yellowish hue, as though withered in a drought.

The jeep stopped a few meters from the bridge. Only after the engine was switched off did Obil notice the eerie silence. No wind blew, no birds sang, no frogs croaked. He could not even hear the roar of the river, whose rapids could normally be heard from a kilometer away.

It looked like a battlefront. There were tanks on the roadside, and along the banks, which were covered with foxholes. Helicopter gunships were parked in a nearby field. Two long lines of soldiers stood on the bridge, pointing their guns over the railings at the water. They wore the leopard spots of the kichwa red, and were so stiff that they might have been sculptures. The only sign of life was a colonel who paced like a metronome behind them. He paused for only a few seconds, gave Obil a long stare, nodded at the sergeant, and then resumed pacing.

"Go," the sergeant said to Obil, nodding toward the river.

Obil licked his lips. The sun touched his face like a hot plate. He swallowed hard, and then walked off the road to the edge of the cliff, and looked down at the river thirty feet below. The water normally ran fast, creating rapids that gained fame as one of the best for adventure rafting. But now, the river stood as still as a pond.

A long canoe was tethered to the bank. Two men in civilian clothes sat at one end of it, while a lieutenant stood at the other end, smoking. Obil did not know the two men, but guessed they were expert divers like him. The soldiers must have looked all over the country for those with the talent to go deep under water. Obil was famous for this. He could hold his breath under water for several minutes. On many occasions, after accidents in the lake, they had sent him to retrieve bodies. But what did the soldiers want him to do? Why were they pointing guns at the river?

What was in the water?

It could not be that they wanted him to look for corpses from an accident. He could see no sign of wrecked cars. The river was not deep. In spite of its strange calmness, its level seemed to have remained the same. If a car fell in, it would be visible. They said a bus, and two vans, had gone in. Others said a pick-up truck as well. Yet, he could not see any vehicle. The only sign that an accident had occurred was the ripped balustrade on the bridge. But how could three (or was it four?) vehicles plunge into the river through that tiny gap?

The accident had been questionable. Reports as to what exactly happened had been contradictory. Witnesses disagreed over the number of cars that plunged into the water. Some said four, and mentioned a yellow bus, two commuter taxis and a pick-up truck. Others insisted they did not see any pick-up. The first lot claimed to have seen a man, a woman, and a girl clutching a teddy bear in the truck, but they argued over its color. Some insisted it was dark blue. Others swore it was white. It had happened at three o'clock in the daytime. How could they disagree over such simple facts like numbers and the color of the vehicles involved?

Obil did not like the mission at all. The soldiers were up to something sinister. If it were a simple search for bodies, a civilian, probably someone from the district office, would have approached him. They would have negotiated payment before driving him all the way here. But the sergeant had not said anything to him, and he had not dared to ask. The drive from his home had been in total silence. Now, they were ordering him to go down there without telling him what to look for.

What was in the river? What made it stand so still?

Obil turned to the sergeant, and met with the dark hole of a barrel. The sergeant smiled, but his eyes had a glint of murder as he nodded at the canoe again. Obil hurried down the steep bank. His legs sank up to the calves in the blackened mud. He was panting, more out of fright than exhaustion, when he climbed into the canoe. The expression on the faces of the other two men only increased his sense of dread. They did not say anything to him, nor did the lieutenant, who stood still at the other end of the boat, chain-smoking.

Obil looked at his reflection in the grey water, which he now noticed moved so slowly, like thick saliva out of an old man's mouth. He could not see anything underneath. The question that had troubled him since they picked him up churned his stomach. The army had its own divers, highly trained commandos who he had once seen in action in a military drill at the lake. Why didn't they use them? Why did they have to frog-march civilians at gunpoint to do the job?

Had the army divers gone in, and not returned?

Something was not right. The accident seemed to be a cover up for whatever the soldiers were hiding under the bridge. Obil's mouth went dry. What would they do if he stumbled onto military secrets? He licked his lips. He would have drunk from the river to quench his thirst, but the grey water looked poisonous. Pimples of sweat clung to his forehead.

"Shall we go in now?" one of the other men asked the lieutenant.

"No talking," the lieutenant hissed. He had a red patch on his lips, a souvenir from drinking crude alcohol.

They sat in the canoe for nearly an hour. It was so silent that Obil could hear the colonel pacing on the bridge. He thought about his own boat. It had an outboard motor. He had purchased it just three months earlier using a loan. He transported passengers across the lake to the islands. He made a tidy sum every day, but he would need another two years to pay off the loan. He wondered if these soldiers would pay him. Whenever district officials hired him, they paid, not a big sum, but as much as he would have earned that day.

The crackle of a radio broke the monotony. Obil looked up

to see the Colonel had stopped pacing. He spoke into his radio. He then leaned over the balustrade and gave the lieutenant a thumbs-up.

The lieutenant stumped out his cigarette. He opened a bag and took out three diving masks. Without a word, he gave them to the divers. He then took out underwater breathing apparatus, and gave each man a set. The other two men had obviously used the gear before. They knew how to dress up in them. One helped Obil to wear the equipment, and gave him a crash course on their usage.

"You can swim," the man ended. "Don't worry too much about these things. They are just to help you breathe and see properly underwater."

Finally, the lieutenant gave them each a flashlight. "You can go in," he said.

The two men went in first. Their dives were orderly and professional. Obil hesitated. He thought the two little splashes they made were too loud. He met the lieutenant's eyes and what he saw pushed him into the river.

The water was surprisingly cold. His muscles tensed. For a few seconds, he could not swim. He sank to the bottom, under the weight of the gas tank on his back. Panic overcame him. He had never been afraid under water, not since he first went in with his father at the age of eight, but the strange equipment made him feel suffocated.

He got a grip of himself just as he hit the riverbed. He held on to a tall boulder with one hand, took deep breaths until he was calm again. The mask enabled him to see in the darkness, but it gave everything a green tint. He saw the other two men had turned on their flashlights, and were scouring the riverbed.

What are we looking for, he wondered.

There was nothing in the water. No wreckage of vehicles. No fish. No frogs. No plants. Just rocks. It then struck him that the river was unnaturally deep. When he had last visited it, the rocks had shown through the surface. Even in the middle of the rainy season, it only swelled marginally. Now, the rocks were about thirty feet under the surface. The riverbed must have sank lower, and sucked more water from the lake. That would explain the unnatural stillness of the water. That such a phenomenon never hit the news meant the soldiers were indeed hiding something.

But what could have caused the riverbed to suddenly sink?

They searched the area beneath the accident spot, went round in a big circle, peered under every boulder, but still did not find anything. Then the two men led the way downstream, though it did not make sense to Obil. The nearly motionless waters could not move a blade of grass. There was no reason for the vehicles to be far away from the bridge.

After thirty minutes of searching in vain, they went back to the canoe, and instead found an army yacht. It had three machine guns and artillery on the deck. There were soldiers in yellow spotted uniforms behind the guns. The lieutenant, the colonel, and a bald man in civilian clothes, stood beside one gun. The civilian wore a dark suit that concealed his short and stout structure.

"This is duck shit," Obil said as he climbed onto the deck. He tore off the mask and the breathing apparatus. "There was no accident."

"Shut up," the lieutenant said.

"What did you see?" the colonel said.

Rocks, Obil wanted to say. "Nothing, afande," he said.

"Nothing?"

"We didn't see the vehicles," Obil said. Then he looked at the other divers and asked, "Were we supposed to be looking for vehicles?"

The other two divers nodded in unison.

"We saw no traces of the cars," one of them said. "Not even of the passengers."

"Nothing?" the civilian said, frowning. His eyes bore deep into their sockets. To Obil, he jerked about like a puppet as if the puppeteer had accidentally touched a string. He tore a notebook from his pocket and drew a line on a page. His hands trembled. "This is the bridge," he said. "This is where the accident occurred." He put a star in the middle of the line. "Now, where did you search?" he stuck the book in Obil's face.

Obil scratched a circle around the star. "Here," he said. "It's the only logical place to search. If the cars crashed in from here," he placed the nib on the star, "then they have to be somewhere here." He drew another circle to stress the area he had already drawn. "The vehicles couldn't have moved anywhere. The river is stationary like a lake of mud."

The civilian snatched the book from Obil and glowered at the page. His eyes darted from the book to the bridge, the frown deepened. His eyes seemed to disappear under the shadows of his brows.

"Where did they take the vehicles?" the colonel said. Obil discerned panic in his voice.

"Who?" Obil said. He felt very thirsty, his mouth so dry that his tongue crackled like a dead leaf. "Who took the vehicles?"

No one replied to him.

"What are you hiding under the bridge?"

Only the lieutenant seemed to have heard. "Shut your mouth," he said, and blew chunks of smoke at Obil

"Go search there," the civilian said, pointing to the western bank of the river, right under the bridge.

"But Afande," Obil said. "If the vehicles crashed in from the middle, how could they move thirty meters over huge boulders to the banks?"

"Just go and search," the civilian said.

Obil turned to the colonel. "Afande," he said. "There is something you aren't telling us. We need to know –"

A gun cut him short. The lieutenant put the barrel on his temple.

"One more word," the lieutenant growled. The safety clicked off. "Just say one more word."

"Leave him alone," the civilian said. "You can ask questions, but you won't get any answers now. First, find the vehicles."

Obil felt the gun leave his skin. He heard the safety click on.

"What are you waiting for?" the colonel said.

The other two men dove in. This time, even though he was trembling inside, Obil dove like the expert he was.

He tried to concentrate on the search. He thought if he did exactly as they told him, he would return home alive. He would wear his new clothes on Christmas and take Amito to dance in the city. That, however, did not take away his fears. They had told him to search, but they had not told him what exactly to search for. The vehicles? What if he stumbled onto some military secret, would they not ensure he never tells anyone? They would kill him. He would never wear his new clothes. He would never propose to Amito.

Unless he escaped. He could swim under water, up the river to the lake. He could easily steal a boat in the night from one of the many nameless fish markets on the shore, and speed away into Tanzania. They would never find him there.

He could make it.

It might mean losing Amito forever. She loved him. She wanted to be with him. If he ran to Tanzania, he might have to forget her. He would try to send word to her so she could join him, but if the soldiers intercepted that message... But if he stayed, the soldiers would surely kill him to protect their secret. He had to go.

He swam fast upstream.

Just as he passed under the bridge, the flashlights of the other two men fell on a metal. They were near the western bank, right under the bridge, where the civilian had told them to search. Obil swam to them, until he was close enough to make out a bus and two vans. According to the witnesses, all three vehicles had fallen in at a particular spot. The first vehicle, the bus or the pick-up, depending on the witness, tore the steel and concrete guardrails and the others followed through the same gap. They should have been in a mangled heap on the riverbed, not in a perfect queue as though parked in a garage.

As he swam around the vehicles, more questions troubled him. How did the civilian know where the vehicles would be? Who was that civilian?

The bus bore no evidence of an accident. No dents, no broken windows, no broken lights, nothing dented. It had come to a stop in the riverbed as it would have done by the roadside to drop off a passenger. He swam in through an open window. No corpses. No passenger luggage. No evidence that humans once traveled in it. He searched the two commuter taxis, but it was a similar case.

There was no mess. Not even the bits of debris passengers often discarded.

They scoured the area around the vehicles, looking under every rock, and still found no evidence of the passengers.

The two men, with gestures, indicated that they were giving up. They returned to the yacht. Obil watched them swim back downstream. He could guess what the civilian would tell them, once he heard about the find. 'Go search this place,' and once they searched that place, they would certainly find something. But what? The bodies?

What if they saw something that the army did not want them to ever talk about again?

Obil turned off his flashlight and swam fast upstream, using the night vision feature of his mask. It was blurry, the green disorienting, but it enabled him to avoid the boulders. Aruri landing site was about five miles away, at the source of the river. He could easily steal a boat from there in the middle of the night, and flee across the lake to Tanzania. If he kept close to the riverbed, the soldiers on the banks would never see him. He had enough oxygen to keep submerged for many miles. In any case, by the time he ran out of gas, he would be very far from the bridge.

He had gone about a mile upstream when he came upon a cylindrical rock. It reminded him of a pillar he once saw in a picture of an ancient Greek temple. It was seven feet high. He swam to it, and saw that a design of strange flowers and fish was carved on it. It could not have been the work of nature. At its foot sat a circular rock, smooth and flat, about four feet in diameter, a teddy bear stuck underneath. Some witnesses had spoken of a girl and a teddy bear in a truck. He turned on his flashlight, and searched the surrounding area, but did not see the truck.

He did not want to know what the two stones stood for, why they were set in the middle of the river. If he did, he could unravel the mystery. But his life was already in danger. Certainly, by this time, they had noticed his escape. By running away, he had brought the wrath of the army upon his head. The soldiers on the banks were probably already running about in a frenzy, searching for him. Maybe the helicopters he had seen grounded earlier were now airborne, darting over the water's surface. Maybe they would fire canons into the river to force him out. They would hunt him for the rest of his life. But if he unraveled the mystery, he might use the knowledge to bargain for his life. If they caught him, he could claim that he was not running away. That something caught his attention and he went on his own to investigate. Maybe they would buy the ruse and thank him for using his own initiative.

He grabbed the teddy bear by one ear and gave it a tug. The circular stone moved a little. He pulled harder. The rock moved again. A hole appeared under the stone. When he pulled a third time, he met resistance. Something in the hole pulled back. He let go of the teddy bear and it sank into the hole. The stone slid away, uncovering a pair of eyes. Yellow eyes. They were not exactly eyes, just two bright shining yellow discs staring up at him.

In a panic, Obil turned to flee. He could not get away. The thing grabbed his legs. Its skin was cold and scaly, like fish. It had human arms, but with umpteen very long fingers. They coiled around him like snakes, and pulled him into the hole. He sank into a large cave. And there he saw the truck, but it could not be a real truck for it was transparent. The thing ripped off his mask. He could not see anymore. He felt it grab the breathing apparatus. In spite of his panic, he took a long breath such that when it tore the equipment off his nose, he was ready.

The thing dragged him a short distance, and then shoved him against a wall. It wrapped something around his body. He felt like a giant snake had trapped him. He could not move his arms or legs. It made him lie supine. Minutes passed. He could not hold his breath any longer. He let go. Water rushed into his mouth, into his lugs, he struggled. Then something long and spongy was shoved into his nostrils, down into his lungs, and he could breathe again. His lungs were full of water, but he was not drowning.

Someone struck a match. It burned bright. He puzzled, for fire and water could not mix. But here was a match burning in the water. Or what looked like a match. It never went out. Behind it was a man. He was stark naked and had an unkempt beard. His eyes were bright yellow discs. His hands ended in a mess of creepy, long fingers, one of which held the match. His toes were webbed. Obil closed his eyes. He thought it was all a nightmare. All he had to do was wake up, and the monster would be gone, but when he opened his eyes again, there it still was. It held a tiny creature that looked like a catfish in one finger. It shoved the catfish into Obil's mouth.

Obil fought back. He clamped his teeth, but the fish forced its way down his throat. He screamed into the water.

The monsterman swam away. As it went down the cave, Obil saw people lying in rows on the floor, tied up in giant green ropes. They were all stark naked. Like the monster man, they had umpteen fingers and webbed toes. They seemed to be sleeping. Something pumped inside their bellies like a second heart. Their chests rose and fell steadily, bubbles escaped from their mouths and noses with each breath they took. Floating beneath the roof of the cave was luggage. He took that to be the passengers' luggage. They floated in little groups - bags alone, clothes alone, purses alone, shoes alone, even coins had their own little pile. He noticed one odd pile of diving gear and army uniforms. The army divers had ended up in this cave.

Then the light went out and Obil sank into a dreamless sleep.

When he woke up, he at once became aware of the metamorphosis that had occurred to him. He had a dozen fingers in each hand, a dozen webbed toes in each foot. He could see in the darkness, but his vision was yellow and blurry. He could not tell the difference between rocks and the people he had seen lying on the floor, but he could hear them. He at first thought he was hearing the chaotic chatter of conversations in a market. Yet he was under water.

We are inside your head and you are inside ours, somebody said that to him. It was a complex sort of telepathy that involved the same mind in different bodies. They had access to his brain, and to his soul, just as he had access to theirs. They had the same consciousness. He knew each of their histories, right from their respective births. They knew his history too, even things that he thought he did not know about, like his birth in a canoe as his parents rushed to a maternity clinic on the mainland. They knew that he was an expert swimmer at the age of four and a professional diver by the age of eight. They knew about his new clothes, and about Amito.

He was conscious of other memories too, of a strange world with a yellow sky, that had no sun, no moon, or land. A water world with only one kind of creature, that looked like catfish, whose reckless activities had caused apocalyptic evaporation. He had memories of travelling through the stars with six siblings in a vessel that looked like a cylindrical stone, in search of a new home, with hundreds of eggs waiting to hatch, and finding this world. Finding his home. As a survival strategy, they had to develop an endosymbiotic relationship with the species they found in the new world, and especially with the dominant species. Humans. These memories and histories did not make sense.

"What did you find?" a voice asked. He knew that voice. The civilian.

He looked around, wondering if the man was in the cave. But how could he be audible under water?

"Nothing," another voice said. He knew that voice too. One of the other divers. "We did not see the cave."

Obil understood what was happening. The catfish was listening to the conversation in the yacht. It had an omnipresent ability. He became aware of the angry truck drivers five miles away shouting at the soldiers to open the road so they could go home. He became aware of the frenzy on the river banks. There were soldiers on every inch of the river, all the way to Aruri, poking the water, searching for him. Helicopters darted about. Boat loads of *kichwa red* zoomed up and down the river. He ignored all these happenings, and focused on the conversation that mattered most to his survival.

"The cave has to be there," the civilian was saying. "It has to be."

Obil felt the divers looking at each other. He could feel the fear in their blood.

"Where are they keeping the bodies?" the colonel asked.

"Who is keeping the bodies?" the diver asked.

"We should pull out those vehicles and see what we can find," the civilian said.

"What do they want with the bodies?" the colonel asked.

"Who knows," the civilian said.

"We should bomb the river," the colonel said.

"Maybe that's what the Americans will do," the civilian said. "They are coming tonight. I'm done here."

Obil went into protective mode. If they bombed the river, it would destroy him. Them. They had to move. The seven creatures, the size of full grown catfish, could fit in the cylindrical space vessel and fly away to safety, but the hundred or so human beings they had transformed could not. They would have to swim upstream, keeping to the bottom of the river to avoid detection, and hide in the lake. It was so deep that they could safely hide at the bottom until the time was right to establish peaceful contact with their new neighbors.

Obil wanted to cry. He would never wear his new clothes again, or propose to Amito. His memories of her, his dreams of a future with her, mingled with the a hundred other memories of loved ones, with a hundred other broken dreams. He could not cry. He felt relief for he had escaped death in the evaporated world. He dreamt of a new life at the bottom of the lake, this was his home now. ✷

A Killing in the Sun

The trial ended, but the firing squad could not proceed. The doctor was missing. After thirty minutes without word of his whereabouts, the sun became furious. It suspected the soldiers were only putting on a show and would release Mande when public interest in the case evaporated, so it tried to execute him.

In defiance to the sun, Mande did not sweat. Even after standing for three hours in the heat, the only sign that it troubled him was the frown on his face. You could mistake it for fear, especially when he eyed the prosecutor who stood directly opposite him.

He loathed the prosecutor's uniform, that plain green shirt of educated officers. The symbol of girly soldiers who spoke English instead of Swahili. The mark of cowards who had no experience in battle. Of fools who returned from exile to assume powerful military positions. Idiots who owed their existence to the President's insane plan of 'professionalizing' the army.

He liked the three judges. They sat to his right, at a desk borrowed from the primary school; the court martial was hosted on its playground. The three giant potbellied frogs squeezed into a tiny desk built for children. Still, they were real men. They were brave fighters. They brushed off the irritations of the terrible sun and appeared to be relaxed. Though they had sentenced him to death, Mande hoped they would let him go. They were true soldiers. Like he was. They wore battle gear, not plain shirts. They also hated the prosecutor and they despised their new roles as judges even more. Mande could see it on their faces, hear it in their voices, smell it in their sweat. Each minute that passed without sign of the doctor increased his hope that it was a trick to save him.

When the President launched his 'professionalization' campaign, he had made it clear that no execution should occur without the public present to witness the eradication of 'bad soldiers.' To prove to the skeptical civilians that it was not a charade, a doctor they trusted had to be present to verify the death of the condemned man.

In the beginning, the whole village would come to watch these court-martials. But when the situation did not improve, when army savagery seemed to increase rather than diminish, most people lost interest. Less than a hundred had turned up to witness Mande's execution. They stood in a horseshoe enveloping the court, waiting for the doctor. But they would not endure the sun for long. A few wore straw hats. Two carried worn-out umbrellas. Mande could see that their patience was wearing out. They shifted about, uneasy, as though they did not know what to do with their feet. Another thirty minutes without the doctor and they would walk away to escape the heat, forcing the soldiers to call off the execution.

The prosecutor could not ask them to wait in the classrooms, for that would be tantamount to dismissing the court. He too lacked the stamina to wait in the sun. His uniform was already dark with sweat. He frequently removed his cap to wipe his forehead with a dirty and soaked hanky. Much sooner than Mande anticipated, he crumbled to the ground like a tree felled by an axe. He lay in the sand, facing the sky, fanning himself with his cap.

Mande's hopes flared. The judges grinned in open contempt. The four soldiers who stood on guard behind Mande sniggered.

With the prosecutor down, the civilians let out an angry murmur. Some began to walk away. Behind them, four army jeeps crouched. The firing squad lay underneath these vehicles to escape the sun. Mande knew they too were not happy with the job. When they heard that the prosecutor had collapsed, they hurried into the jeeps, anxious to get away.

Mande watched his enemy the way a vulture eyes a starving child. He was a little dismayed when the prosecutor stood up again, but it refreshed his hope when he noticed that the officer's knees wobbled like a blade of grass in a strong breeze. Something other than sweat shone on the man's face as he scanned the horizon for the doctor. Something that Mande recognised as panic.

He followed his gaze, past the vehicles toward the school. The hospital lay somewhere behind the gaunt and abandoned classroom blocks. Even from this distance, the wounds of war were clear on the walls. The doctor had to come through these buildings. Being a Saturday, not a pupil was in sight. Neither was the doctor.

In frustration, the prosecutor cursed and lit it up a crumpled cigarette. He paced about, puffing, wiping sheets of sweat off his face. One by one the civilians began to leave. Soon, there would be no one left but the soldiers. And then, even if the doctor did show up, there would be no execution.

But just as Mande started to bask in the thought of cheating death, someone in the crowd shouted, "Daktari!"

Mande looked up to see a figure in an oversized white robe whizzing through the classroom blocks on a bicycle. For the first time since they arrested him, he realized he was going to die. He turned to the judges, to plead, but the sun shoved a ball of fire into his throat, blocking his airway, making it difficult to breathe. He did not see any hope in the eyes of the judges. He only saw pity. He licked his lips with a parched tongue. His mouth tasted like stale oranges.

Reluctantly, the firing squad stepped out of the jeeps and cocked their guns. The civilians scrambled back into a horseshoe around the court, jostling each other for a good viewing spot. The prosecutor's strength returned. His knees no longer wobbled. He threw his cigarette onto the sand, and slowly crushed it as he grinned at the judges in triumph.

"Let's proceed," he said.

The four guards took Mande by the arms. He did not protest. They escorted him to a tree fifty meters in front of the court martial. The only tree in a radius of two miles. It stood sixteen feet high and had a trunk twelve inches thick. Tiny branches grew out of the tip of the trunk and stood naked against the blue sky. Only a few dust-caked leaves struggled to survive on the withered bark.

Each step Mande took seemed to make the tree shrink. In the past year, more than two-dozen soldiers had died here. Executed. It had become a symbol of the President's 'professionalization' campaign. Mande wondered why they chose a tree hidden behind a school. There was a very big mvule near the barracks, visible from a mile off. It would have been a better symbol. He knew seeing that tree everyday would've stopped him from pointing the gun at that priest.

When Mande stepped into the thin shadow of the tree, his legs froze. A wave of dizziness made him sway like a drunk. He thought he could hear the roar of a fast running river. He stared at the trunk as though he expected it to burst into flames and talk to him. The guards did not push him to keep walking.

Less than a minute later, the doctor dropped the bicycle and ran the last few paces to the tree. He stood uncertainly before the prosecutor. He looked ready to kneel and ask for forgiveness.

Sweat dripped off his chin. Mande thought he could hear the drops splash on the ground.

The prosecutor turned to Mande, "Before you die, we can grant you anything you wish. Anything within the law."

Mande could not speak, so he pressed a fist against his crotch, pointed a finger at the ground and made the sound of urine jetting into the sand.

Puzzled, the prosecutor asked, "Is that all?"

Mande nodded. He gulped. Thirst tore at his throat. He wanted a glass of crude waragi. But that's what he killed the priest for. It would not look good if he asked for it.

The prosecutor nodded at the guards. They took Mande a few paces away from the tree. He stood with his back to the court and eased his bladder for a long time. The sound of urine jetting into the sand reminded him of the priest.

When he finished, the four guards used white ropes to tie him to the tree. He blinked, and then squinted. His cap had fallen off. The sun shone fiercely right into his eyes, as if his punishment was not enough.

"Remain a man," one guard said, securing the last knot. "Don't cry."

The guard placed the cap back on Mande's head. Now the condemned man could see again, and he saw that the judges were not seated anymore. Everyone stood still, everyone but the six armed soldiers marching through the haze of heat toward him.

"Safe journey," the guard said, walking away.

"A priest," Mande tried to say, but the sun scorched the words before they could leave his mouth. His lips merely parted with a thirsty, sucking sound. He had to say his prayers without a priest. He closed his eyes. Hail Mary, full of grace—and that was all he knew. He tried again. Our father, hallowed be thy heaven—and he could not continue. His head dropped in a resigned bow. There's no priest. I killed a priest. I cannot pray. God cannot forgive me.

No. He recalled the Sunday school tale about the thief crucified with Jesus. *God can forgive anyone, but how do I ask for forgiveness? How many Hail Marys should I say?*

He opened his eyes. They were brimming with tears. He noticed that his fly was open, revealing a clean pair of white boxers. He had bought them just last week after he got his salary. All those people were looking at his pants! He wanted to zip up, but could not. His hands were bound. He struggled with the ropes, in vain, and that released the tears.

A whistle blew. He looked up, in time to see a blur of soldiers pointing guns at him. He felt it more than he saw it, the fingers snaking around the triggers, squeezing, the bullets shooting out of the barrels — he jumped for cover.

For several seconds, he thought he had indeed escaped. He had the sensation of falling into a deep hole, somewhere far below the ground where the firing squad could not get him. He thought the judges had secretly dug this hole to hoodwink the prosecutor and the civilians.

His feet touched soft ground. It was so soft that he looked down in curiosity, and saw that he was standing on water. Like Jesus. It then struck him. He was in the world of the dead. In a kind of alley. Ahead and behind lay deep darkness. Light from an unseen source lit up two gates. One stood on his right — a big, red, stone beauty. The other lurked on his left — a very small and ugly door made of rotting wood. Both were ajar.

He was about to go through the red gate when he remembered another Sunday school lesson. 'The road to Hell is smooth, big, and beautiful.' So he turned around and walked through the small, ugly door. Into a very narrow street that reminded him of Shauri Yako, the famous trading centre of a dozen mud buildings with grass roofs. This street looked exactly like that stinking corridor where, two evenings before, he had killed the priest – only, this one seemed endless.

At first, he did not see anybody.

There had not been anybody when he found the priest urinating against the mud wall. He asked the man of God for a coin to buy a glass of waragi. The robed man refused. So Mande pointed his gun at him, not to kill, only to threaten. And the priest said, "If you want the drink so badly, why don't you point your gun at the barmaids?" Before he could reply, Mande heard the whoosh-whoosh sound a gomesi makes when a woman is running. He turned to look. Alas! In that movement, he pressed the trigger. An accident. He did not mean to shoot the priest.

Then, he noticed the women in the shadows, toothless old crones in hooded black cloaks that reminded him of a cassock. In the dim lights of dusk, they appeared as a dozen replicas of the woman he saw running away when he pointed his gun at the reverend. The sole witness of his crime. He became aware of the skulls piled against the mud walls, conjuring the picture of that building they set up to remember the war. The useless building the President said was for peace. As he watched the skulls, and the hags, the evil of the place rose out of the ground like thin mist.

"Welcome!" One crone grinned at him. The hood pressed so tightly against her head that he feared it would eat into her skin. Her face was severely pockmarked. Her teeth were funny, not like human teeth, more like long shards of yellow bones. He cast another glance at the skeletons and started to think of cannibals.

"No, don't go away." The witch continued to grin, closing in on him as he backed towards the gate. "You have nothing to fear..."

The words his wife told him a long time ago, just before the war broke out, to convince him not to flee the country. He stayed, and she died two days later when government soldiers stormed their home. They tied him up and forced him to watch as they killed her and his children. A week later, he roamed the streets with a band of rebels.

He darted out.

He dashed for the other gate. The big, beautiful, red gate. It would not open. The crone with the pockmarked face stood behind him, grinning, saliva drooping from her wrinkled lips. In panic, he burst into a run. He fled down the tunnel. The woman chased him. Her cloak made the whoosh-whoosh sound. The same music the gomesi had made. It prompted him to run faster. The darkness seemed to part around him, as if someone kept a searchlight on him. He desperately searched for other gates. Saw none. His fleeing footfalls echoed. The whoosh-whoosh of the witch's flapping cloak pursued him, tormented him.

Suddenly, a big church stood right in front of him. It looked exactly like the one he went to when he was still a boy, long ago when the world was so peaceful and innocent. When all he wanted to be was a soccer star. He ran towards the church and he had a strange sensation that he was running towards that golden age of his life, that the years were falling off and he was becoming younger, and younger, until he was just a little boy racing his brothers to Sunday school.

The whoosh of her cloak reminded him that it was an illusion. That he had just been in a corridor between two mud walls, pointing a gun at a peeing priest. He ran faster.

He outran the witch. He sped into the church. The pews were full. A priest stood at the altar. Only this priest was not preaching. He was urinating as the congregation watched in silence. The witch gained on him. Her whoosh-whoosh sounded louder than ever. He had nowhere to run. She leapt on his back, and they tumbled on the aisle. She had him. A darkness overwhelmed him.

He had the feeling he was on the ground, his face felt hot, something heavy was pressing him, and someone... The witch? Only she sounded different, was saying, "His heart is still beating."

He opened his eyes but could not see clearly, just vague shapes and shadows in the brilliant world, but he knew he was back under the tree. Its branches hung above him like strange dark clouds in a white sky. He felt more than saw the doctor stepping away, but heard him say, "Amazing. All those bullets and he's still alive." Some of the bullets had severed the ropes binding him to the tree and he'd fallen into the sand. He lay on his back. "He'll be dead in another minute."

"I can't wait another minute," another voice said.

A vague shadow stepped into sight. It looked down at him. From its aura he knew it was the prosecutor, and he was pointing something at him. A pistol. It flashed three times. Mande did not feel the bullets hitting him, but he knew they drove into his skull.

"Check again."

The prosecutor's shape moved away, and the doctor's aura flooded in until his kind cloud was all that Mande could see. Its warmth comforted him.

"A priest," Mande said. "Please bring me a priest."

But the shadow moved away from him, and once again all he was looking at was the shapeless, withered branches of the tree.

"He is now dead."

Mande heard the lone footsteps of the prosecutor hurrying away, his boots crunching the sand. Everything else stood still. Though Mande could not see it, he knew the prosecutor was avoiding the eyes of the true soldiers. He knew they were glaring at him. He heard a car door open, the imposter zooming away. Then he heard the faint shuffling of dozens of feet, the civilians departing. Within a minute, he remained alone with his fellow soldiers. Their shadows gathered around him. He could feel them staring down at him as though they did not know what to do with his lifeless body.

Mande wanted to smile, to tell them that the trick had worked. He was not dead. They had saved him. But he instead said, "Please, bring me a priest."

They did not hear him. They just stood there for a long time, very still, in silence, their caps off their heads. He knew they would give him a three-gun salute when they finally lowered his cheap coffin into the grave.

He wished they could know that all he wanted was a priest. ✷

The Doctor's Truck

The street was empty. The sun was fierce. Mirages simmered on the dirt road. Some of the town's folk were inside their shops, hiding from the heat as they waited for customers. Most were idling under the cool trees behind the buildings, playing omweso board game, drinking beer to quench their thirst. Dr Okot's lips, cracking from the heat, ached for something icy. His throat, choking with the taste of dust, felt like an old, rusty pipe. His vision was a little blurred, his palms slick with sweat, as he steered the truck to Salama Hotel.

He always thought of Wemo as 'the red town', for dust coated the buildings and vegetation, giving it a surreal color. The town had cropped up just ten years ago, in anticipation of an economic boom from the new hospital. But like most charity projects, the hospital failed to deliver on its promises, killing the dreams of the town. There were about ten buildings scattered along the dirt road. Most were incomplete. The red brick walls had no plaster. Only one building had paint, a sun bleached yellow. At two stories, it was the tallest structure in a radius of thirty miles. It accommodated Salama Hotel. He visited it every day, after lunch when there were no patients at the hospital, for a cold beer.

There was nobody inside the restaurant bar. Dust coated the tables and chairs. The only sound was the hum of a refrigerator, which increased his thirst.

"Osinde," he called, rapping on a table.

"I'm coming, doctor," a man shouted from the backyard. "Wait."

The doctor sat on a bench, drumming the table with his fingers. Nearly two minutes passed before the waiter, in a dirty white shirt, walked in through the back door.

"Good afternoon, doctor," he said in Swahili.

"It's a hot day," the doctor said, his voice hoarse. "I pray for rains."

"Don't mention it," the waiter said. "Should I get you the usual?"

Dr. Okot nodded. "I hope it is iced today."

"Yes, yes," the waiter said, as he gave the door of the fridge a tug. It did not open. It had a fastener and a padlock. "Ah sorry. Last week someone stole a beer so I put this on when I'm in the kitchen. A minute. I'll get the key."

The doctor cursed. He glowered at the waiter, who disappeared through the back door and ran across the backyard to a grass-thatched hut, which served as the kitchen.

An engine ignited. The doctor frowned.

His pick-up had been the only vehicle in Wemo, until six days ago when a mzungu appeared with a bigger truck, a double-cab, that had the blue logo of the United Nations. But the foreigner's car was parked behind the kitchen. Dr. Okot could see its bumper. The sound of the engine came from the street. It had to be his pick-up igniting.

A carjacker?

He parted the curtains and peered out of the window. The driver's seat was empty, yet the engine revved, and then the car sped away in a whirlwind of dust.

The doctor ran into the street, just in time to see a little girl crossing the road. The split second in which it happened stretched for an eternity. She turned her head to the car in surprise. Her mouth opened to scream, but no sound came out. A cloud of dust rose, obscuring his view. He heard the vehicle slamming into her little body.

The pick-up then reversed, broke out of the dust cloud, and screeched to a halt at the same spot that he had parked it. The dust faded away, revealing a yellow bundle spread in the middle of the road. He had not noticed the color of her dress before, and now he hoped that yellow thing was not the girl.

"What happened?" a voice asked.

It took him several seconds to recognize it as the waiter. Now, he became aware of the people stepping out of the shops. He could hear feet running from the backstreets. He could feel anger stirring in the street when they saw the yellow bundle on the road. He wanted to feel that anger too, but his insides felt hollow. His stomach was just a bag of frightened air.

He staggered to the girl. Her eyes and mouth were wide open, the scream crystallized on her face forever. Brain seeped out of her smashed skull. Blood soaked her uniform. He checked her pulse. Nothing.

"Mangulata's daughter," the waiter said.

The doctor knew her too, though he could not recall her name. He had treated her of malaria just a week before. He could still remember her smile, which shone even as the fever burned through her body. He sat down beside her, and watched her blood flow away in rivulets, like earthworms wriggling away from a danger only they could perceive.

He sensed the mob gathering around him, in silence, hardly casting any shadows. Their eyes burned his flesh with accusation. Vengeance flowed out of their pores, and dripped onto him like molten plastic.

I did not kill her, he tried to say. The words stuck in his throat, a rusty pipe clogged with muck, chocking him.

He looked over his shoulder, at the car. There were several men behind him. He saw the car through their legs. It was out of focus. Their pants and shoes were sharp in focus. Beside one leg, a club dangled. Beside another leg, a machete gleamed.

They would clobber him to death.

A woman started to wail. Her voice pierced the air like a whistle.

He staggered to his feet. There were about a dozen people around him, each had a weapon. The unspoken rule on roads was that if you knocked down a pedestrian, you do not stop, for a mob will lynch you in vengeance. Instead, speed away to the nearest police station and report your crime, or simply vanish. This mob had not yet descended on him because they knew him. He had stayed when other doctors had fled, after the hospital project had failed, and that had made them see him as a part of the community. That was the only reason they had not already clobbered him to death.

But now they thought he had killed the girl, they would forget the good he had done for them. They would forget the sacrifice he had made by staying to keep the hospital alive. They would want his blood in vengeance.

Tears clouded his vision as he staggered away from them, toward his truck. Why he was going to it he did not know. They gave him way, but he knew they were behind him, following with their weapons raised. They were only waiting for a spark, for someone to strike the first blow...

The car drove itself, he wanted to tell them. He could only gasp.

No one else had seen it. No one would believe him. He went down on his knees, bowed his head, closed his eyes, and waited for the first blow to strike him. To break his skull open just as the car had broken open the girl's skull. He hoped to pass out with the first blow.

"Don't kill him!" a voice shouted in English, in a strange accent. "He didn't do it!"

Dr Okot looked up, to see a white man's head poking out of a window on the first floor of the hotel. Their eyes met, and he thought he saw a flare in the mzungu's eyes, like sunlight bouncing off a metallic surface. They had first met the previous day at the hospital. His name was Grant. He said he was in town researching local opinion about a project the UN planned to implement in the area. Another project bound to fail, Dr. Okot had thought when he had heard Grant's pre-conceived ideas of what the locals wanted.

"I saw everything!" Grant shouted. "Don't kill him!"

Most people in the mob did not understand English. One man did. He was the only law enforcement officer in Wemo, an elected official who thought of himself as the president of the town. Dr. Okot had forgotten his name because people just called him Chairman. He had been at the helm of the village council for over fifteen years.

"Wait," Chairman said.

The doctor wanted to turn around, to get a good look of what was happening behind him, but he remained on his knees, waiting. The mzungu vanished from the window. Seconds later, he came running from around the building, panting.

"It was not him," he said. "I saw it."

He had braided his beard, three locks dangled on his chin. His hair was the color of sand. The sun had burnt his skin red. His eyes had a green tint that unnerved Dr. Okot, who could not imagine a human being with green eyes.

"You did?" Chairman said.

Dr. Okot felt a headache coming.

"Yeah. I was on my window. I happened to be looking out. It's the weirdest thing I've ever seen. I thought it was a trick of the sun, but it was real. I saw the doctor stop, and he got out of the car, he went into the restaurant. There was no one in the car. But when the girl appeared on the road, the car drove itself and hit her."

Several seconds passed. There would have been total silence if it were not for the woman wailing. Her melodrama drove a knife into the doctor's gut.

"Was he in the restaurant?" Chairman asked the waiter.

"Yes," the waiter replied, after a moment of consideration. "I left him there to get the fridge keys from the kitchen. I was gone for only a few seconds. I did not see what happened, but I left him sitting in the restaurant. When I came out to the street, he was standing by the road, not inside the car." He paused for another few seconds before adding, "Maybe the mzungu is right."

Dr. Okot felt the immediate danger ebbing away. The mob would not pounce on him just yet. He had two witnesses on his side, but no one could explain the strange behavior of the truck. Everyone present thought of something, but no one said it aloud.

Juju.

#

The doctor abandoned the car on the street. He could not bring himself to even touch it. He would leave it there until the police came. The station was over thirty miles of bad roads away. They could not possibly come that day.

He took the rest of the day off. He longed to talk to Amito, his wife, but she was still at the primary school, where she taught English and Mathematics. He wanted her to hear it from him before she heard it from anyone else. He tried calling her, but he could not get through because of the bad phone network. He thought about walking the five miles to see her in person, but the heat sapped all his energy. And the news would travel faster than he could walk.

He collapsed onto a rocking chair under a mango tree in his backyard, brooding, drinking beer to calm his nerves. When he heard an engine, he stiffened, anticipating the sound of metal slamming into flesh. He closed his eyes, trying to dislodge the image of the yellow pile on the road from his mind. The car stopped in front of his house.

It then came to him that it must be the mzungu, who owned the only other car in the village. Dr. Okot did not want to talk to anybody. He wanted to be left alone. But before he could instruct the maid to turn away the visitor, she showed Grant to the backyard.

"That is not a good idea," the mzungu said, looking at the beer bottle.

Okot smiled politely. The urge to yell about how wazungu always thought they knew what was best for Africans nearly overcame him. He wanted to rave about the failed hospital project, to tell Grant that it was a grand example of how 'stupid white men with a superiority-save-Africa complex' try to force their views on other people. He wanted to say a lot of nasty things, but the words did not come. He took a sip from his bottle, and looked away, out of the chain link fence, at a herd of cattle grazing in the fields.

"It's a ghost," Grant said. "And I can help."

Okot turned to him, "Ghost?"

Grant shrugged. "Well, you people call it ghost, but it is something that can be explained scientifically. There are metaphysical forces –" He pulled a DVD and a neatly folded sheet of paper out of his pocket. "Look, I have a friend. He is a ghostbuster. He can help you."

Dr. Okot did not touch the things the mzungu held out to him, but he saw that the paper was a flyer for an investigator of paranormal activity.

"On this DVD, you'll see him at work. He can get rid of the ghost that has taken control of your car."

Okot did not respond. His eyes clouded as he stared at the flyer. It had stripes of yellow. There had been only one yellow stripe on the road.

"Here is my Ugandan number," Grant said as he scribbled a number on the paper. He then placed the flyer and the DVD on Dr. Okot's lap. "Call me if you don't want your car to kill more little girls."

The mzungu walking away.

#

That night, Dr. Okot and Amito lay sleepless in bed. Heat smothered the room. They kept the windows open, and the fan running, but that did not stop sweat from seeping out of his pores. The sheets clung to his skin. He got out of bed, took a cold beer from the fridge, and staggered out of the house. He sat on the doorsteps and watched clouds dashing around the moon.

Amito joined him a few minutes later. She had a cold bottle of water. They did not talk for a long time. An owl hooted. A soft breeze blew, cooling them down, and Okot wondered why it had not blown into the room through the window.

"Why do we live here?" Amito broke the silence.

The question had troubled Okot since he saw the yellow bundle on the road. When he first came to Wemo Hospital, shortly after it had opened with a lot of fanfare, the money had lured him. He earned four times above the government rates. Then the project failed, because patients did not turn up. The hospital had to retrench most of its staff. He was the only doctor left. The idea had seemed a good one, setting up a hospital in a region that did not have functional health centers, but it ignored the culture and history of the locals. He knew that they preferred traditional medicine, which he and the Western donors had been quick to dismiss as primitive and backward, until he witnessed a herbalist curing a boy of cancer. He had then questioned everything he had learnt at school, everything he had been socialized to believe. He had thought of a radical project, in which the hospital would embrace traditional medicine, as well as the cultures and sciences of the place, rather than impose an expensive and foreign health system. His employers had not yet bought into the idea. Now, he wondered if it was worth it. The locals were happy with their medicine men. They did not need him, or the hospital.

"Let's get away," she said. "I hate teaching in that school. I want to teach pupils who are interested in learning, not pupils who only think of taking cattle to drink water." He wanted to retort a reminder that learning to take cattle to drink was probably better than learning about Cinderella, but he only took a swig of his beer. "I don't want our children to grow up here."

He placed a hand on her shoulders. She buried her face in his chest.

#

A little after sunrise the next morning, the maid awoke Okot. He stepped out in nothing but a bathrobe, to find visitors waiting in his living room. He knew Chairman, who sat between two elderly men. He recognized one, from the costume of bark cloth, as a mganga.

"How is your morning?" Chairman said.

"Fine," he replied.

"This is her grandfather," Chairman said, nodding at the second old man. "This mganga told him it's her father's spirit. You see, her mother has been sleeping with her uncle, who isn't the heir. That made her husband's spirit very angry. So the mganga wants to prevent the ghost from using your car again."

Why my car? Dr. Okot wanted to ask, but he only swallowed saliva to wet his throat.

"It's still in the street," he said. "I'll never drive it again."

Chairman nodded. Without another word, the three men rose, shook his hand, and walked out. At the doorway, the girl's grandfather paused.

"We shall bury her today," he said. "We have to do it quickly because of the manner in which she died. Please be there so you can ask for her forgiveness."

#

The funeral started at three. A large crowd gathered at the bereaved homestead, which housed six families and had a dozen grass-thatched huts with mud walls. The family necropolis lay in a garden behind the homestead. Banana plants soared above the graves like phantom guardians, blocking out the heat of the sun. The mganga stood beside the priest, whose sermon accentuated the sorrow and the oppressive heat. Dr. Okot and Amito stood at the mouth of the grave, along with the girl's mother.

Just as the priest started to say a prayer, a scream chilled the afternoon.

"The car!"

Okot turned to see a woman running up the road toward the homestead. In the distance behind her, a plume of dust whirled toward the mourners. He could hear the whine of an engine. His pick-up.

The burial turned into pandemonium. People ran in all directions, screaming. Within a minute, only a handful of the mourners remained, waiting in resignation as the car sped toward the homestead. Amito held Okot's hand in desperation. Her fingers dug into his flesh. A breeze rose, making the banana leaves rustle, like wings of demons, accentuating the silence that gripped the graveyard.

The car stopped about twenty meters away. It was empty.

"I was wrong," the mganga said. "It wasn't the girl's father." He turned to Dr. Okot, and pointed a scrawny finger. "You must have knocked someone else dead, and now the ghost is haunting your car."

Dr. Okot's knees went weak. His tongue went dry, his lips cracked. He became aware of eyes glaring at him. Sweat broke out of his skin. A drop ran down his face, tickling him like the finger of a witch.

"I've never knocked anyone," he said.

"Then why is a ghost driving your car?" Chairman said.

Amito started to cry. Her fingers dug deeper into Okot's flesh, until he was not sure whether it was sweat or blood trickling down his palm.

"You must have sinned somewhere," Chairman continued. "You must be running away from bad things you did somewhere. All your friends left when the hospital failed, why did you stay? Why do you choose to live in such a village? Why don't you return to the city? That's where all educated young men want to live, not here."

Amito's crying went up a notch. Okot hugged her, to comfort her, hoping she would not feel the fear that gripped him. He could not be sure anymore if he had never killed a person. Over the years he had run over many animals, sometimes in the night when he could not tell exactly what it was he had knocked over. Maybe one was a human.

"Confess your crimes," the priest said. "Turn to God, and he will vanquish the evil haunting you."

The breeze turned into a strong wind. The leaves screamed. A dust devil danced in the distance, as though to confirm the presence of a ghost.

It was his car. He had to do something, to stop it from killing more children.

He looked deep into his wife's eyes, an apology struggling to come up his throat. He could not say anything. He wriggled his hand out of her grip. She let him go. His knees wobbled as he walked out of the banana plantation. The wind threatened to knock him over. Blackjacks clung to his pants as he cut through the high grass. He ripped off his coat and tie, and threw them into the bush. Amito stopped crying.

Fire. A thought blazed in his skull. Destroy the car to destroy the ghost.

He staggered into the homestead, into the nearest kitchen. He picked an axe off the wall, and a burning piece of wood from the stove. Then he stepped onto the road, and faced the car. Chicken blood from the mganga's ritual streaked it red. There were pig-bone necklaces and other fetishes that the mganga had hung on its bonnet and roof. The headlights blinked. The indicators flashed continuously, like multiple eyes winking at him. Mocking him. He could hear the sound of the lights. It made him think of the ticking of a clock. He bit his lips, bracing for the fight with the supernatural.

He felt the weight of the axe, felt the heat from the wood. His palms were slick with sweat. He felt his energy drain, and wondered if he would be able to burst open the fuel tank.

"You can't burn it here," Chairman shouted.

Dr. Okot turned to see him standing a safe distance away, cowering behind a hut, clutching something in his hands. Even from the distance, the doctor recognized the sheep-tail whisk, a talisman to keep away ghosts and evil things.

"Take it away," Chairman said. "Burn it where there are no people. Not here."

Dr. Okot had heard of a Christian pastor who had convinced a shaman to stop practicing magic. He set the shrine on fire, but the moment it started to burn, human-like creatures the size of small rats jumped out of the flames, killed them both, and ran amok in the village, razing several homes before vanishing into a forest. Something similar might happen if he torched the car in the village. He had to take the vehicle away.

But how could he drive it? The ghost was in control.

There was a garage thirty miles away, in Tororo town. He could call for a tow truck, but it could take the whole day to arrive. In that time, the truck might kill another girl.

As he glared at the car, a movement in the distance caught his eyes. Someone was riding a bicycle at high speed, coming toward him. The rider got close enough for him to recognize the mzungu. Okot had done an internet research of the ghostbuster that Grant had recommended. They seemed to be a genuine firm with clients mentioning them in more than three different blogs. He had also watched the DVD, which showed the investigators trapping a ghost and kicking it out of a house. He had given it a lot of thought, but did not see the practicality of them coming all the way from America just to exorcise his truck.

Grant peddled fast towards Okot. He did not steer away from the truck. He showed no fear of it. He rode past, not even glancing at it. He kept his eyes on Okot.

"Hey," he said as he brought the bicycle to a stop in front of Okot. "I was just riding by, doing my daily exercises, and I saw the commotion."

The doctor did not know his heart was pumping so fast until he tried to speak.

"I can help you," Grant said. "My friends are experienced. Look, your witchdoctor's blood and pig bones have not done anything. You must understand that the metaphysical forces you call ghosts are not supernatural. They are elements of nature, like the wind, and they can be manipulated with technology."

"How?"

Grant jumped off the bicycle, and moved closer to Dr. Okot and began to whisper, even though there was no one near enough to overhear him.

"Can you raise twelve million shillings?" Grant said.

"Twelve million?"

Dr. Okot swallowed hard. Although he was a well-paid doctor who made thirty million a year, he had a string of relatives who depended on him. He was paying fees for three brothers at university, and also educating four of Amito's siblings. To buy the truck, he had saved for many months and had taken a bank loan, which he was still paying back.

"It's only about five thousand dollars," Grant continued. "The money is not for me. It's for the ghostbusters. It will pay for their air tickets, accommodation, and such things. Surely, you can afford that. But don't think about the money. Think about the girls your car will kill."

All Dr Okot had to do was say yes, wipe out all his savings, and the ghost problem would disappear. But why was the mzungu whispering? He wondered.

"Sorry," Dr. Okot said. "I don't have that kind of money, but thanks for the help anyway. I have a solution."

Grant's eyes fell on the piece of wood. A thin trail of smoke rose out of it.

"You can't destroy a ghost with fire," Grant said.

"No," Okot said. "But I can destroy its home."

"Don't be stupid," Grant said. "My idea is better."

"Thanks," Okot said. "But leave me alone. This doesn't concern you."

"It doesn't make sense for you to burn a car and then buy another one which will simply be a new home for the ghost. Look, you seem like a nice guy. You are a do-gooder. You sacrifice your life to serve poor people. I really want to help you. I earn a ridiculous salary as an expatriate. Five thousand dollars is loose change for me, so I can help you. Tell me, how much can you raise? I can top it up for you."

That is when Dr. Okot began to suspect that he was dealing with a con. Why would a stranger offer him free money?

But then, he thought, why would an expatriate aid worker want to swindle him? He looked again at the foreigner, at how his green eyes sparkled in the sunlight, and he realized that he did not know anything about him. Grant claimed to work for the UN, but he had offered no ID. Dr. Okot had not asked for one, maybe because of the UN logo on his truck. Now, he was confused. He thought it strange that Grant carried a ghostbuster's flyer and DVD with him. As Dr. Okot thought more about it, he recalled that the blogs that mentioned the ghostbuster firm had no more than ten entries each, and the last post in each had been made over a year ago.

But how had the car driven itself? And if Grant was behind it, why would he drive all this way in a vehicle worth more than five thousand dollars, just to rob a rural doctor of a few pennies? It did not make sense.

He turned his attention to the truck. He stared at the blinking lights for a beat, and then without another word to the mzungu, he marched to the pick-up.

"Don't be a fool!" Grant said.

Okot clenched his fists, tightening his grip on the axe and on the burning log. He grit his teeth, bracing himself for a clash with the ghost. Sweat dripped off his beard. His knees were weak, cramps worried his thighs, but he kept going. If he stopped, he would lose courage. A strange force propelled him forward. He reached the car, and without giving it a second thought wrenched the door open.

He expected something to happen, the vehicle to explode, the ghost to materialize, but nothing happened. He dumped the axe and the burning wood onto the bed of the truck, hoping the flame would not die out during the drive, and then he climbed behind the wheel.

He waited for the ghost to strike him. Nothing happened. The seat felt too warm. His palms were slick with sweat. His fingers trembled as though he was in the grips of severe malaria. He turned on the ignition. To his surprise, the engine started.

He looked up, and saw Grant riding very fast back to town. He concentrated on the task at hand. He held his breath, shifted gears, and stepped on the accelerator.

He drove with apprehension, still expecting the ghost to take over the truck again. He felt like a mouse in a cat's game, just before the cat settles down for dinner. He turned off the road, and crawled over a narrow footpath that led to a swamp, which lay in a forested valley a mile away from the nearest homestead. Destroying the evil in such a place would not harm innocent people, he hoped. He bumped through the calf-high undergrowth, twisting and turning to avoid trees.

Then, the engine stalled. He turned the key. Nothing. The truck could not move. The ghost was back in control.

He punched the steering, and screamed, "No!"

The engine sputtered to life again. He stared at the ignition, but the key stayed on the off position. The truck began to move, maneuvering to make a u-turn and head back to the village. *To kill more little girls.*

He flung open the door and jumped out. He fell, scraping his elbows and knees, and nearly got run over. He ignored the pain, he ran to snatch the axe off the bed of the truck. The fire had fizzled out of the wood, but that did not matter anymore. If he could not burn the car, he would drown it in the swamp.

First, he had to stop it.

He swung the axe, aiming for the rear right tire, but the truck had already made the u-turn and was rolling away from him. He missed and instead hit the taillights. He swung the axe again, hitting the body. The truck must have realized he was trying to stop it, and it suddenly jerked forward. There were too many trees blocking its path. It had to keep turning to avoid them, so when it increased speed, it could not turn fast enough. It rammed into a tree. The bonnet flew open.

The damage was not too great to stall the car. It reversed, but now the doctor had a good aim of the rear left tire. His axe cut deep. The tire deflated with a hiss. He raced to the front and split the left tire open as well.

Now, the car could not escape. The engine revved, smoke spewed out of the pipe, but it only wobbled and drove into another tree, and then it was stuck.

Dr. Okot approached it. Cautiously. Something dangled out of the busted rear lights. It looked like an eye attached to a tube. He went down to his knees for a closer look, and that is when he realised it was a camera. It looked like a webcam.

There was no ghost.

He searched the truck and discovered more cameras behind the other lights. Was the vehicle being controlled by remote? He went to the bonnet, searched for several minutes, until he found a strange black box, cleverly hidden beneath the radiator. A multitude of wires attached it to the engine.

His suspicions now made sense. It had to be Grant.

He had heard of the US Army using unmanned planes, called drones, in combat, but he had also heard that the technology was too expensive. That this Grant had quickly wired up his car, and tried to extort only a few thousand dollars from him, indicated that the technology was cheap, and easily usable.

#

Dr. Okot called Chairman. He talked frantically, explaining the technology he had found in the car, but the connection was so bad the conversation kept breaking up. He sent a text message instead. *I found evidence. There is no ghost.* The mzungu is behind it. Arrest him. He did not get a response. He tried calling again, several times, but he failed.

He ran to the nearest homestead, where he borrowed a bicycle and sped back to Wemo.

#

When he sped into town, sweat soaked his clothes. His chest burned with lack of air. A crowd armed with pangas and rungus stood in the sun in front of Salama Hotel. Silent. Waiting.

"Chairman is with him in his room," the waiter said, as the doctor dismounted from the bicycle.

Dr. Okot ran up to Grant's room.

The door was open. Chairman and a dozen men stood around Grant, who was bound to a chair. On the table, was a machine that had remotely controlled the truck. It had a steering wheel, a gear lever, a speed meter, and under the table, pedals for the breaks and acceleration. There was a laptop too, on which several windows were open, showing the views from the cameras attached to his car.

"Look at this," Chairman gave the doctor a blue ledger book. "He has been doing it for a long time."

Dr. Okot leafed through the pages. The man had kept meticulous records. He had travelled to many parts of rural Africa, "infecting" vehicles of high-income earners with his ghost, and then tricking the owners into giving him money to exorcise the ghost. His victims numbered in the hundreds. Now, Dr. Okot understood why he asked for such a small sum. When totaled from all his victims, it would be in the hundreds of thousands of dollars. Maybe millions.

Dr. Okot looked at Grant who, though trussed up had a smug

smile, the arrogance of a man who knew his time was up. But who knew that the moment Chairman handed him over to the police, he would bribe his way to freedom.

#

They frogmarched Grant to a giant mvule tree, the village court. Within a few minutes, the family of the dead girl and half of the village had gathered for a session. It was the lowest court in the country's judicial system, and it had no jurisdiction over murder cases, but they found the mzungu guilty of murder and extortion. Later, when the police came, Chairman would claim that he had failed to stop the mob.

The dead girl's grandfather cast the first stone. ✷

Lights on Water

He did not know how to talk to his daughter. Silence sat between them like a concrete wall. She hugged herself on the seat beside him, arms wrapped around her legs, chin pressed into her knees, eyes fixed on the window, watching the city fall away as they soared into the sky. She wore a green loincloth and a bra fashioned like calabashes. Her hair was braided like spikes, twinkling with green and yellow beads. Her skin glowing in the soft lights of sunrise, gave off a faint smell. She needed kilo ointment to hide her tawny-brown hue with a sooty shade. But now that she had started to menstruate, she used ova lotion to keep clean. The mixture created an awful stench. He could not open the air vents while in flight. He had to endure the odor, just as he had endured her tantrums, her accusations that he was not her father.

He did not know why she agreed to accompany him on this trip. Did she also believe it would heal their relationship? Did she think he was going to show her a new way to permanently darken her skin? Was it simply the allure of leaving the city for the first time in her life? He could not read the answers off her face. She kept it turned away from him. He thought she was watching the wings of the bruka. She used to enjoy it as a child, swaying her arms to imitate the flapping, and now he wondered if she was thinking about that time when they were a happy family, before her mother died, before she was old enough to understand that her skin was a shade lighter than that of everyone else.

Traffic thickened as they neared the city gates. His speed dropped. He joined a long queue of farmers floating to the Banana Gate, one of the hundred on the sky-high wall imprisoning the city. He flashed his royal pass at the check point. He was on a special assignment from the Emperor. The abasura waved him through without questioning why he had a passenger, or searching his ornithopter for stowaways. Outside the wall, the other brukas dropped to the ground, to join the thousands of workers harvesting millet in the sprawling farms. His was the only aircraft heading for the wilderness. On three occasions the abasura stopped him, but they let him go without a fuss on seeing his royal pass.

As they flew over the wild, he prepared for the patrols. The previous week, he had witnessed them vaporising a man who tried to escape from the city. He turned on the vidisimu and sent a broadcast of his royal pass. They picked it up at once. Though he could not see them, they hit his bruka with a blue light, signalling him to stop. He pulled the wing lever to halt the flapping, and then stepped on the flybrake. The ornithopter hovered just below the clouds. An officer's face appeared on the vidisimu screen. Afande Moti, so fat he did not have a neck.

"How did you sleep, Songo?"

"I slept very well, afande. Have you eaten breakfast?"

"I'm full," the officer said through his teeth. "Who is she?"

"Kimi. My daughter. She is my model today."

Songo held his breath. His royal pass allowed him to take models out of the city. But while the Emperor wanted him to paint a demon in a river, there had been no mention of a human in the picture. If Moti checked with the palace, they might ask him to explain his decision to take a model. He hoped the ambiguity of the assignment would save him, but it could also send him back to jail. Maybe this time they would execute him.

"Fly safe," Moti said. "Watch the skies. There will be a storm later."

"Asante, afande," Songo said.

The vidisimu went off. The blue light vanished. Songo's chest relaxed with a sigh. Kimi cast him a questioning glance, maybe now suspecting that it was an illegal trip. For a minute, he had doubts about his plans to smuggle her to the beach. Even with a royal pass, he was forbidden to access it. According to official dogma, the sea was Hell, the abode of the devil, a place for the dead, the source of evil. Upon it the people of Jok were taken to be enslaved. Nobody was allowed to visit it. Only a couple of artists could. Not him. They banned him from it. They would kill him, and Kimi too, if they found them there. But he had to take the risk, to take her to the seaside where she would start to unlearn everything. He had to show her the truth, if she was ever to accept and love him as a father.

He could start her re-education in unrestricted locations, where they might slap on him a token day in jail if caught. Places like the Valley of Flowers, which resembled a rainbow on the ground, or the Whispering Forest where trees sang a ceaseless tune, or the Pink Lake whose waters glowed as though painted by a perpetual sunset. But such places lacked the magic of the four lights. Its sight was like a taste of the forbidden fruit. Kimi had to experience the magic. He could think of no other way to make her love him again.

The ornithopter flew just below the clouds, giving her a view of the enchanting wild, the sprawling jungle, the rivers sparkling as they snaked through the brilliant green. Other than in paintings and pictures, she had never seen the natural world before. He glanced to check if the sight thrilled her, but whatever she felt did not show through the mask on her face.

About twenty minutes after his encounter with the patrol, he dove into a valley and skimmed a river that flowed into a thick forest. The trees arched over the water, forming a tunnel. He folded his wings to prevent them from entangling with the branches, and used the emergency battery, which could not sustain more than ten minutes of flight, to land on a rocky bank. He did not open the doors. He instead took out his camera and captured images of the river that he would use later to paint. He would wait in the forest for a while, and then emerge from the other side, flying close to the ground to avoid the scanners, and sneak off to the ocean.

Kimi cast an inquisitive glance at him again. He gave her a big smile, and he tried to tell her to admire the beauty, but the words stuck to his throat like a lump of frozen fat. She turned away from him and pressed her face on the window. She watched flowers glowing in the half-light, swarms of fireflies moving in enchanting formations, moths and birds encircling the aircraft. He could see a dim reflection of her face on the glass. It was not enough for him to guess her thoughts.

After thirty minutes, he restarted the engine and flew off. The forest grew thinner until it dissolved into grassland. Less than a minute before the engine would crash, he turned it off and switched back to the solar battery. He kept close to the ground, below tree level, to dodge the abasura scanners. They flew over a herd of zebras, passed a couple of giraffe, floated over elephants, and sped along with a lion chasing down an antelope. Now, on the dim reflection on the window, Kimi's eyes grew larger in amazement, a smile lingering on her lips, threatening to erupt. It lit a warm glow in his chest.

They neared the coast. He waited for the blue light to hit

him, for the patrols to stop him. Nothing happened. His muscles relaxed. He had beaten them. Yet again. He had used the same trick before to take his wife to the beach.

He went round a hill, and Kimi gasped. Her lips parted open in wonder. One moment, all they could see was a large expanse of tall grass and trees. The next, to their left was a steep cliff with a pencil thin waterfall dropping into the sea, creating a mighty roar and a misty ambience. On their right was the ocean, the waves crashing against the rocks and sand. The bruka glided to an outcrop of rocks where thousands of white birds were perched, basking. Kimi screamed.

"Are those demons?" she said, in a frightened whisper, speaking for the first time that morning.

He did not respond at once. It would take her a long time to unlearn the poison they had fed her since she was a little child. First in the temples of Jok, then at school, little drippings of deadly data that made her hate herself, that made her doubt if he was her father.

"For all the years I've been coming here, those birds have never hurt me."

"For years," she said, as though trying to understand the phrase. "You did not report it to the abasura." The disappointment in her voice turned the morning into ice.

"They know about them."

She was silent for a while, maybe finding the information unbelievable, and then she spoke, "They should be exterminated."

Songo steered the craft toward the shore. He wanted to give her a close feel of the birds. Maybe if she heard their sweet cooing, and touched the little ones, and felt their fluffy feathers, she would not think of them as demons. Before the bruka could touch the ground, anger flared in her eyes.

"Are you going to land here?"

Beaten, he took the bruka back up. She slunk into silence again, maybe thinking about the colorful birds in her books. They represented angels. White birds did not fly to the cities anymore. People had killed the last one of them two hundred years back. The phrase 'white bird' was now associated more with fable than with reality. They only appeared at a certain time of the year. It made Songo wonder where they stayed the rest of the time. It could not be inland, for they would be killed. He thought they lived somewhere beyond the four lights, which he could now see in the horizon.

Kimi had not yet noticed them. It was hard to see them at once. They were merely four dots in the distance, each the size of a fist, in a straight line. Only a few knew of their existence. No one ever talked about them. No painting of the ocean ever depicted them, yet they were a permanent feature just like the waves. No one knew what they were, or what lay beyond. The Ministry of Geography claimed there was nothing offshore, just water. The Ministry of Spiritual Affairs claimed that the sea was Hell. Myths and legends talked of worlds on the other side.

The most famous was in the Book of Life, in the tale of Mojech who led the people of Jok out of slavery from a land called Hamerikah. The Book never talked of who enslaved them, but people interpreted it to be white creatures that were half human and half bird. Their king, Wasiton, raided Jokland and took slaves in great ships. They worked for him for a thousand years until Jok sent Mojech to free them. King Wasiton refused to release them, so Jok struck Hamerikah with a hundred plaques until he succumbed. Unable to sail the ships, Mojech parted the waters of the sea with his magic staff and the slaves walked back home. It took them forty years.

Songo did not believe the Book. He thought Hamerikah was a fiction, like Heden, Kaanaan, Heziya, and Zayon. But the Mojech story intrigued him. If it took them forty years to trek across the sea, how long would a bruka take? A couple of weeks? A day? A year?

He used to think the four lights were pieces of metal gleaming under the sun. One day, his bruka broke down, and he waited for rescue until night. Then he saw that they were lights. He thought they were Pyramids with ten thousand families living in each, the collective glare from the windows making each shine like a single pearl. A week after this discovery, he tried to fly to them. He sneaked off the coast and flew low over the water to avoid the scanners. After twenty minutes, the lights were still four tiny dots in the horizon. He begun to think they were a mirage. Before he could fly further, a bruka gunship came after him. They would have vaporised him if he had not quickly sent them his royal pass. During his trial he claimed that he had wanted to paint land from the point of view of a demon. He could have been executed, but the propaganda machinery needed his talents. He instead served a year in jail.

"Here is a nice spot," he said, as they flew over a stretch without seaweed.

"It's too white," Kimi said.

"It won't hurt you," he said. "It's just sand."

"What is sand?"

"It's – it's like the soil on which our food grows... but of a different texture."

She did not say anything. He thought she was struggling to

understand it all, for she had never touched the natural ground. She did not know the texture of soil. All her life she had lived thousands of feet up in the air.

The bruka landed with a jolt. He jumped out. He gulped in fresh air, a relief after her odour. The jungle was alive with bird music, which played in perfect sync with the waves. Kimi put a frightened foot down. She pulled her leg back, maybe surprised by the ticklish feel of sand, maybe thinking it was bad luck that the first time she steps on the ground is on a place painted with the devil's color.

On his first day at the beach, he had imagined that sand was a type of water and that he would drown. He had clung to the ornithopter as his mentor laughed. He barely knew the old man at that time. They had met only a few months before. He had come to the beach legally, as an apprentice. It had felt strange walking on sand, the squelchy touch, the sound of it crunching under his feet, the thought of it being ominous to walk on something so white. The artist should be fluid like the wind, the old man had said. Go anywhere you like, even to Hell, or else your imagination will never fly. He took the advice and became more than just an apprentice. Songo never found out why the old man had no family, but something of a father-son love flourished between them.

He did not laugh at Kimi. He pretended not to notice her fear.

He set up the easel on the shoreline. The water lapped at his ankles. He looked at pictures in his camera. The Emperor wanted a monster to leap out of the river and snatch an angel on a mango tree. Songo thought a human prey would be more frightening. He looked away from the camera, at the coastline. He had been banned from the seaside ever since he tried to reach the lights.

Whenever he got a commission to paint the beach, they asked him to do it from memory. He longed for that time when he would spend days on the beach, the wind on his face, the sun on his skin, as his brush flew over the vidicanvas. Now, he wondered if he should make the river flow into the sea. He could make the demon creep out of the ocean, go up the river, to a tree where an angel sat eating a mango. Or maybe he could have her sitting on the white sands of the beach, not an angel but a girl.

"You will be vaporised if you ever depict people at sea, or if you ever draw those four lights," his mentor had told him.

"Why?" he had asked.

"Who knows?" the old man had replied. "Just never do it."

He heard Kimi. She was walking towards him, her eyes on the sand, maybe puzzled that she was making perfect footprints. She had a smile, the first time he had seen her smile in two years. Dimples blossomed on her cheek. The sun licked her face, uncovering memories of the happiness they had before her mother died.

"It feels," she searched for the words to describe it and then, laughing, said, "Squishy?"

"Take a swim," he said.

The smile vanished from her face. A frown appeared, shocked at his suggestion. She could not swim in public. Water washed off the kalo and exposed her true color. All her life she had lived in fear of being found out. One day, shortly after her mother's death, fed up with the fear, she stepped out of the diiro without the kalo mask. The neighbors shrieked in terror, as though she were a monster. Their faces twisted in disgust, they spat, they puked. "What have you smeared on yourself?" they yelled at her. "You look like a demonic red worm!" Rage deformed their faces.

"We shall vaporise you for blasphemy!" The next week, Songo had quietly moved to a new Pyramid, to a new set of ten thousand neighbors.

She never left the diiro without her kalo mask again, even though it gave her a bad scent whenever she had her periods and had to use it with oya. The odour made her repellent. No child wanted to play with her. She got angry with him. "Who is my real dad," she kept asking. The Book said that children inherited their skin color from their fathers. Since all humans were descendants of Habram, everyone had the same sooty shade. Why then was she a tawny-brown?

He wished her mother was still alive to help him handle her. She had died two years before, during her second pregnancy. He never knew what killed her. He suspected that they had terminated her for refusing to swallow kalona, which pregnant women were required to ingest monthly. They claimed it immunised the unborn against a plethora of disease, but his mentor had told him the truth. It gave the baby a dark hue. It ensured everyone was the same shade of charcoal. While pregnant with Kimi, Kama had secretly refused to swallow the tablet. She delivered from her diiro, later explaining to the abasura that it had happened too suddenly for her to go to the otyat. At birth, unlike other newborns with sooty looks, Kimi had a pale skin. Over the years, her skin had darkened into a tawny-brown. Songo feared the ointment had done it.

"Is it safe?" Kimi asked, her eyes searching the beach, scanning the forest with its incessant music, prying the clouds for a spybruka, which the abasura used to watch over the city.

"No one is here," he said. "No one will see you."

The frown did not leave her face. She peered into the water, fear shimmered in her eyes.

"What about demons?"

He laughed. He stripped off his robe and remained in his loin cloth. He ran into the water, and swam far out. He found a colorful shell. The official dogma said all sea creatures were pure white, the color of evil, because salt water bleached everything.

"See?" he said, giving her the shell. "Isn't it beautiful?" Afraid, she refused to touch the shell. "It's all a myth. Demons don't exist."

"Then why do you draw them?"

He shrugged. "They want people to think that the ocean is evil."

"Why?"

So that people don't get the idea of leaving Jokland, his mentor had said. But he could not explain it to Kimi. She had not yet discovered the lights.

"I don't know," he said. "I'll ask the Emperor the next time I see him."

"But, they do exist!"

"Have you ever seen a demon in a camera picture?"

She looked at him wide-eyed. She shook her head almost imperceptibly.

"Isn't it suspicious that you see them only in paintings? Three days ago, the Emperor told me that there is a new monster. He described what it looks like. I have to bring it to life. I've never seen it. He has never seen it. Even the priests have never seen it. They will see it after I draw it." He shrugged again. "The pay is good."

She stood still on the sand, watching the waves, as though waiting for a demon to dive out and gobble her. He thought how much she looked like her mother, his beautiful Kama, his first model. Her portrait had earned him the Emperor's respect. In it, she blinks, and then her lips part slowly into a smile, to reveal the gap between her front teeth, her dimples glowing, deepening, her eyes twinkling, mirroring the face of whoever looks at the picture.

Songo turned away from the little girl, forcing the image of Kama out of his head. He threw the shell back into the sea, picked up a pencil and started to sketch.

Fifteen minutes passed. Kimi crept towards the edge of the water. He stopped drawing to watch her. She tested the ocean with her toes, and then let the waves wash over her ankles. The kalo drained from her skin, turning the water black like monster blood. She waded in until it reached her knees, a black trail behind her. The kalo dissolved into the sea. Soon there was no trace of it, just a tawny-brown girl swimming in bliss. A wave struck her. She fell, and vanished. He held his breath, but then she jumped out screaming in delight. Her laughter, the high-pitched squeak of pure happiness, filled the morning with the promise of a sunny day.

Songo painted fast as she played in the water. He sketched with a pencil, drawing a still picture at first, tracing out the forest, the river, the shoreline, the waves, the clouds, and then using the motion brush to animate the images in an endless loop, the trees fluttering, the river flowing into the sea, the clouds sailing, the waves licking the shore. Within an hour, he had the background ready. Kimi had not left the water since she got in. Next, he began to sketch the demon rising out of the sea, but then his pencil found a life of its own, and he ended up with an angel, a tawny-brown angel.

Before he could give it wings, the voice of reason whispered.

Erase it.

Instead he brought the angel to life. It exploded out of the water with a mighty splash, its mouth opening in a silent scream of delight as it shoots into the air, and then splashed back in, vanishing for a few seconds of calm, before leaping out again, in an endless loop.

The Emperor's propaganda machinery would never use the painting. It would only lead to Songo's vaporisation, but Songo did not destroy the angel. He looked out into the sea, at the lights shimmering just above the waves, and he knew how to finish the picture. Using the zoom function of the motionbrush, he could make the lights grow larger until they became Pyramids, with a myriad of tawny-brown angels dancing in a celebration never seen inside the dystopian cities.

After two hours of splashing about, Kimi came out of the water, her arms full of colorful shells. They sat under a shade for breakfast. Gonja spread with odi, warm milk in gourds, slices of pineapple. They ate in silence. Kimi watched the ocean all the time. Songo recalled how the waves had captivated him, that day a lifetime ago with his mentor.

"What are those?" she asked.

"The waves?"

"No. Those four things, over there," she pointed.

"Oh. You've finally seen them," he smiled.

"Are they metal?"

"No. Lights."

"Lights?"

"Yes."

"What's making them?"

"I don't know."

A brief silence cropped up. She did not know about his term in jail, which happened a year before her birth.

"Maybe that's where demons live."

"If demons were in the ocean, you'd be dead by now."

A cloud swept over her eyes. He thought she was frowning. She ate in silence for a while, her eyes fixed on the lights.

"Do they ever go off?"

He shook his head. "I think it's the border of another place, maybe not of hell and demons, maybe a place very much like our own." He paused, and then added, "Maybe a better place."

"Heziya or Hamerikah?"

"Who knows."

"Maybe I could swim to it."

The first time he saw the lights, he too had thought of swimming to it, but the old man had given him a piece of wisdom. It's better to imagine what place that might be, than to go over and find it is actually hell. He wanted to tell Kimi the same thing, but he had not listened to his mentor. While serving his year in jail, he wondered what the old man had been trying to tell him. Was it a warning? Was it the wisdom that knowing the truth does not bring happiness and so it is better to fantasise rather than investigate? By then the old man was long dead. He could not get clarification. The quest for the truth had nearly cost him his life. Knowing about kalona had destroyed his family. The truth was dangerous. Still, every time he came to the beach, he wondered how he could beat the bruka gunship and reach the lights. Every time he saw a pregnant woman, he wondered how to tell her about kalona.

"It's too far out," he finally said. "You can't swim to it. Maybe if there was a way to travel underwater, you could reach it. If you try to fly, they will vaporise you. And if you tell anybody what you have learnt today, they will vaporise you."

After they had eaten, she pulled out an umbrella and lay on the beach, to shield herself from the strong rays of the sun. She dozed off. Songo continued to work. He intended to leave the beach before noon, the abasura would check on him in the forest about that time. He could complete the painting from memory. He only wanted to stay long enough to bring the idea to life.

A blast of sirens told him it was too late.

He turned to see a dozen fat men in black zooming above the treetops, their ornithopters fitted onto their bodies like dresses. They steered with their shoulders, while their hands held flash guns, the long kind that looked like bananas.

Kimi shot to her feet, frozen, unable to run into the bruka to smear kalo on her skin. The abasura would be on them any moment. Songo caught her eyes, and he could see the glint of anger, the accusation that he had tricked her, brought her out here into the sea, lured her into the water, and let the abasura find her without her mask on.

One officer landed. The others stayed in the air, flying in circles like a swarm of bees, their guns aimed at father and daughter. Songo did not recognize Moti until he took off his helmet. The wings folded behind his back. The wheel between his thighs crumpled into a ball, which moved into a pouch under his protuberant belly.

"Have you eaten yet?" Moti said in greeting, smiling.

"She's my model," Songo said, loud enough for Kimi to hear. He hated the tremble in his voice. "I wanted a demon that looks like a girl, that's why I painted her."

The officer glanced at Kimi, who stood rooted like a baobab

tree. Disgust distorted his face. He spat, and it was as if the spittle hit Kimi's face. He did not break his pace as he waddled to Songo.

"We should have checked her after we discovered her mother's non-compliance," he said. "Someone will pay for that oversight."

It confirmed what Songo had feared all along. They had killed Kama. They had discovered she was not swallowing kalona. Her second pregnancy had been a mistake. After they got away with Kimi, they had decided not to have another child, but one night she forgot to drink the matindi soup, and four weeks later she missed her periods. They thought of an abortion, but they had gotten away with it the first time. Maybe they could beat the system again. Unfortunately, when she went to the otyat to treat a bruka accident wound, she did not come out alive. They said she suffered from internal bleeding. Now, he knew for sure. They had killed her for refusing to swallow kalona tables.

Moti stopped a couple of paces in front of Songo.

"You learnt nothing in jail," Moti said.

"Look," Songo replied in a husky voice, pointing at the four dots in the horizon. The officer followed his finger, cautiously, squinting, and then he saw the lights. He turned back to Songo with raised eyebrows. Apparently, he already knew about them. Unable to speak, Songo turned the easel to show Moti the painting, the angel jumping out of the water and a light materialising into a Pyramid.

Moti's eyes grew wider. His pupils flared with an intense brilliance, his skin became so tight that Songo feared it would break. His lips parted with a click.

"There are no Pyramids in Hell," Moti said, breathless.

"It's not Hell," Songo said. "It's all lies."

"Shut up." Moti raised the gun a little higher pointing

it at Songo's chest. "I could send you to Hell right now, you blasphemous infidel."

Songo's eyes fell on the weapon, on the red bulb that emitted death rays. His hope flickered. If they were to be killed, that bulb would have already flashed.

"Follow us," Moti said, and leapt into the air. He hovered above Songo, still aiming the gun at them.

Silently, Kimi climbed into the bruka. Songo packed up his tools, his unfinished painting, and in the next minute they were in the clouds. Two abasura flew in front, three on either side, four behind. Kimi applied kalo on her skin as they flew over the wilderness, more out of habit than to hide her color. He told her about kalona, the truth about her skin. His voice low, barely a whisper, crackling with pain, as he rationalised the decision he and Kama had made. He tried to paint a glorious picture of them rising against the system, but instead of revolutionary rhetoric, it sounded like the petty experimentation of drunken youth. She did not look at him. He saw her image in the window, tears leaving tawny-brown tracks on her cheeks. She did not wipe them off. The silence returned, thicker than ever before.

An hour later, they entered the great city. They soared high above the clouds to avoid the pandemonium of the metropolis, where millions of ornithopters swirled about in chaotic formations. It took them nearly half an hour to get to the middle of the city, and then they swooped down into a valley that housed the University of Understanding, the place for prisoners. It had three Pyramids no taller than a thousand feet, each a different color, built in a triangle around a black building, said to be the first temple of Jok, supposedly built ten thousand years ago when Mojech had just returned from slavery.

Inside one of the Pyramids, as they followed Moti through a long corridor carpeted with synthetic leopard skin, Songo held Kimi's palm. It was warm, slimy with kalo oil, damp with sweat. She did not flinch as he had feared. Instead, she squeezed his hand tight, and he knew that she was afraid. He could feel her pulse - a buffalo stampede.

"It'll be alright," he whispered. The confidence in his voice surprised him. He thought it would have come out husky, reflecting the miasma of the impending doom that gripped him.

"I love you, daddy," she said.

Tears pricked his eyes. Words came to his throat, declarations of love, pleas for forgiveness, assurances that they would live happily ever after, but none of it spilled out of his mouth. Nothing but a groan. It left the taste of bile on his tongue. He squeezed her hand so tight that she cried in pain.

"In there," Moti said, nodding at a blue door.

It had no writings on it, but Songo knew the room it led to. A black chamber bare of furniture, with murals depicting the Emperor's dogma, the first place prisoners entered on the journey to change their minds, to make them understand. It increased Songo's hope. If they were to be killed, they would not have bothered to bring them into this black room. He put his hand over Kimi's shoulder, to usher her through the door.

"Not her," Moti said. "Only you."

Songo pretended he heard not heard. He hurried on through the door, as though that would save them from the inevitable. Two officers wrenched her off his hold. He did not let go. He hugged her. She wrapped her arms around his neck, so tight he feared she would strangle him. They clung to each other, until Moti punched him in the face. An explosion of light. A sudden silence. Next thing he knew, he was on the ground, supine, Kimi vanishing through the door, her screams bouncing off the murals, and then there was darkness. And silence.

When he regained consciousness, he was back in his diiro. His family and closest friends were gathered in the kisenge, sitting on goatskin mats, drinking mwenge from large calabashes, a sign that seven days had passed since her death. Paintings of Kama and Kimi now hung on the walls. Candles glowed, lending warmth to the chill of the sunset. The chatter of conversation came to him as though from a long way off. He wondered if he had been in a coma for seven days, but if so, he would have woken up in a bed, not on this three-legged stool. He must have turned into an automaton of some kind, a sleepwalker, with a living body but a dead brain. He must have spoken, sung at her cremation, and scattered her ashes into the clouds, but he could not recall any of that. And now that he had awoken, he did not think about her. He thought about the four lights in the ocean.

Silently, he left the mourners and wandered into his studio. He found his unfinished painting on an easel. The lights wiped off, the angel erased, leaving the beach empty, the river flowing in silence into the sea. Maybe the Emperor had commissioned Soma, the only other artist capable of bringing imaginary creatures to life, to finish the task. He understood it as the reason they kept him alive. Only the two of them were able to paint monsters and make it look like the work of a camera. They would keep him alive until they found a replacement. Now he also knew why his mentor did not have a family, and why he had never talked about the past. The Emperor needed people like them. They were essential to the propaganda machine. They had probably given him time to mourn Kimi, maybe in line with the official cause of death. They would not want it known that she had visited the ocean, or that she was a shade lighter than everyone else. They would wait for ten days, and then quietly take him back to the University of Understanding, to spend many years in solitary confinement, a propagandist slave bringing monsters to life for the benefit of the system. The old man must have succumbed to a similar fate.

As he looked at the unfinished painting, the idea that had gripped him at the beach returned with such vividness that he picked the pencil and started to sketch. He worked the whole night and completed the painting just before dawn. Instead of an angel, a girl jumped out of the water in an endless loop. Kimi. Her last moments of happiness immortalised. He added colorful fish and shells playing with the girl. The four lights zoomed out from the distance and materialised into Pyramids, with millions of little girls playing in them. They were not all tawny-brown. He created the illusion that each had a special shade of her own. Green, blue, yellow, red, a rainbow of people. At the top, he titled the painting The Rainbow Sea, and at the bottom he wrote, Kalona - the face of sadness.

He hid the picture and slept through the day. At midnight, as the family held the last funeral rituals, he sneaked out disguised as a cleaner. He spotted the abasura watching his apartment, but they paid no heed to the old man waiting to catch a public bruka back home. Ten minutes later, he broke into his brother's printing factory, and by morning he had made three hundred thousand copies of the painting, each no larger than a page from a little girl's school book, but each clear enough, vivid enough, powerful enough to bewitch the beholder.

He packed them into three huge boxes, and lugged them into

a transport ornithopter. He flew away just as the first workers arrived for business. Hopefully, they would not notice the missing bruka until he had carried out his revenge. His first stop was Ojoma district, where the middle class lived. He waited for a good strong breeze, and then he emptied one of the boxes. The vidipapers fluttered in the air, and the wind carried them to hundreds of Pyramids. They flew into windows, landing on breakfast tables like newspapers, or they just floated about waiting to be plucked out of the air.

He sped to the Black Flower suburb, where the lower classes lived, the uneducated, the casual labourers, the poor. The spybrukas were now hunting for him, but they would not know which bruka released the painting until he did it again. He quickly emptied the second box and sped on to the third suburb, where the intellectuals and artists lived. Half way there, they finally picked him out of the millions of brukas. The blue light lit up his craft. He kicked out the third box, and was glad to see its contents scatter in the wind before a death ray vaporised it.

He had a smile in those final moments. Thousands of copies of the painting had already found their way to citizens. Maybe someone had already uploaded it to the netweaves, and tens of millions of people were watching as Kimi played in the ocean, as the four lights turned into Pyramids full of happy girls, full of a rainbow of deliriously happy girls. Maybe it would spark off the awakening. ✷

A Wife and a Slave

Kopet sat on the papyrus bed, watching his wife sleep. He had not touched her in five years. The last time he tried to kiss her, she had reported him to the abasura and they had jailed him for three days of hard labor. He ogled at her breasts. They rose and fell with her breathing. She snored lightly, oblivious to the noise of the waking Pyramid, to the crowing of electronic roosters, the flapping of ornithopter wings, the blaring of angry horns. The sun flowed in through cracks in the window, making her face glow with a love she could no longer give, filling the room with the warmth that she had failed to provide.

The wine had made him oversleep. He wanted to take a bath and rush to work, but he could not bathe himself. His wife had to do it. He tugged at the goatskin blanket to awake her. It slid off her body. She did not stir.

"Akello," he said.

She did not respond. He grabbed her shoulder, and shook her. Still, she did not awake. Her skin was so smooth it felt like shea nut butter. She once had a light color, a golden brown like fried chicken, but she had used Kalo lotion to darken it into the fashionable, pure black of coffee. It gave her a glossy texture, a perfect look, like the surreal models in the magazines. His fingers ran over her skin, causing desire to rush through his veins like the rapids of the Nile. But he quickly withdrew his hands to stifle the temptation he felt rising in him. He did not want another three days of hard labor.

He crept off the bed and tiptoed to the bathroom. He locked the door, masturbated, and then took a quick shower. He walked back to the bedroom a short while later, towelling his body, she was awake. Panic showed on her face. She fell on her knees.

"My husband," she cried. "Please forgive me. I overslept. Why didn't you awake me?"

He hated that she no longer called him by name, that she knelt whenever they talked. He hated that she was no longer his lover. He wanted to tell her that he had enjoyed bathing on his own, but such a statement could send him to jail.

"You needed a rest," he said, forcing a smile. "But you can still dress me."

He sat on a three-legged stool. She hurried to a giant reed basket to choose his clothing. He eyed her with a mixture of hatred and longing. She was naked. Her ebony hue glowed in the warm beam of sunrise. Her lips were thick and inviting, her nipples fat and juicy. Though she had four children, she still had the voluptuous curves of a teenager. The sight tortured him. He could ogle, but not touch.

He glared at the mural opposite him. It covered every inch of the wall. He blamed it for destroying his marriage. He often wanted to rip it off, but that would send him to the firing squad. The mural depicted what was supposed to be life in Africa before the Europeans came. Kopet wondered if it really had been like this, if wives had washed and dressed up their husbands the same way mothers fussed over children, if sex was strictly for procreation. Unlike the pictures in his childhood, this mural had motion, like a silent movie in the endless loop of an irritating commercial, a thousand different movies playing at the same time on the same screen. Instead of decolonizing the mind, as the Emperor claimed it would, it enslaved the people. It depicted women with unnaturally long necks, men with weird heights and warrior looks. The faces were pure black with ghoulish white teeth and white eyes. It enforced the idea that Africa had a single identity, a single language, a single culture. Whoever painted it did not know that they were promoting stereotypes, and the misconceptions and misinformation that the Europeans had of Africa. Maybe they knew, but they still pasted the propaganda on every wall in every household to keep a firm grip of power. The greatest lie they told, the one that turned Kopet into a seething volcano waiting to erupt, was that romance and sex for pleasure was not African culture. His wife did not question the mural. With religious fanaticism, she obeyed its instructions on how she was supposed to live her life.

She brought him a bark robe and loincloth. After she had dressed him, she gave him a goatskin bag and a straw hat. He thanked her and hurried out to work.

"What will you eat," she said as he vanished through the door. "Milk and katogo?"

"Surprise me," he said, walking briskly through the living room to the garage.

"But you must tell me," she said, following him. She covered up her nakedness with the blanket. "Please, my husband, what food should I bring for your breakfast?"

"Milk and katogo," he said.

She stopped following him. He walked into the garage. Four ornithopters gleamed in the darkness. They looked like eggs with wings and wheels. His was the yellow one, the smallest. The biggest, brown in color, belonged to his wife. The two green ones were for the children. He flipped a button on the wall and the front door whirred as it slid open, letting in the brilliance of the sun, revealing the rush hour madness outside. Tens of thousands of brukas hovered about, some returning from night shifts, others heading out for work. The traffic abasura were overwhelmed. The air was so thick with flyers it seemed impossible to get out of the confusion.

Kopet slid his bird out of the garage. A solar engine in the tail enabled him to fly with closed wings. Most of the brukas stuck in the confusion were older models. They had no engines. Their twelve-foot wings made it difficult to navigate out of the jam. Kopet needed very little space. He steered the machine downwards, staying very close to the surface of the building.

His home was about two thousand feet above the ground, roughly situated in the middle of the Pyramid, which he shared with five thousand other families. These skyscrapers did not look like their ancient namesakes. They were gigantic versions of the peasant huts that once graced rural Africa. They were called Pyramids because the Emperor believed he was the reincarnation of Tutankhamun, and his Bito Empire was the new Egypt.

The traffic was less heavy at about fifty feet off the ground. Kopet increased speed. He skimmed the treetops, keeping low to stay clear of the jam, until he was out of the city. He then soared into the skies and opened his wings to gain maximum speed. He shut down the engine for he loved to peddle. It was the only exercise he had to keep fit.

He reached his workshop at seven. He loved it there, a secluded place behind the hills that formed a natural wall around the city. His nearest neighbor, a fish factory, was over a mile away. He loved the reclusive atmosphere, the sound of birds and insects, of the wind in the trees. Sounds which could no longer be heard in the cities. He loved that his workshop was on the ground, that he could smell the soil after a rain, and that he could choke in dust during the dry season. It was an outmoded building, constructed using red bricks, with a corrugated iron-sheet roof. It reminded him of his childhood, of life before the Emperor's madness, of the love that once flourished between him and Akello.

Kopet had inherited the shop from an old man whose entire family had vanished in the war. Being an orphan in a refugee camp, he had formed a grandson-like relationship with this old man, who taught him about art and sculpture. At the time the old man died, shortly after peace had returned and they were trying to start a new life, a small town flourished around the shop. But then, about fifteen years back, the Emperor built his Pyramids and everyone went to live in them. The town died. The bushes grew tall, swallowing up the abandoned buildings, wiping off the road, enclosing Kopet's workshop in a sea of reclusive bliss. The only visitor he had was his wife. She brought him food twice a day. She once asked that he abandon the old fashioned place and set up his workshop in a Pyramid within the city, but he told her that he was holding on to memories of his foster grandfather. He did not tell her about the secret hole beneath the floor.

That morning, the moment he stepped out of the bruka, he knew that someone had invaded his hermitage. A windowpane was broken. Had a burglar had come in the night?

Once inside, he pulled a string drawing the curtains and filling the room with daylight. He checked the cash box, which he kept in the back room. It was intact, the little money and cheap jewelry was all there. Frowning, he looked around. Nothing seemed to be missing. Clay artworks sat on the shelves, statues and sculptures stood on the floor, half-done pieces were on the tables, everything was as he had left it the previous day. Everything but the broken pane. Maybe a bird had crashed through the glass?

Kopet examined the window, and the shattered glass on the

floor. That is when he saw the stone. It was not a bird. Someone had broken the pane with the stone. Was it a burglar? Why then was nothing missing? Had someone discovered his secret hole? He inspected the green shelf that hid the trap door. Since he opened it regularly, he could not use the dust to tell if the intruder had moved it. He was certain his secret was intact. If someone had discovered it, the abasura would have already arrested him. But what did the broken window mean? Did the burglar find nothing worth stealing?

He gave up the mystery. He switched on an electric broom. It sucked the broken glass and flushed it through pipes to a garbage pit in the backyard. Then, he saw something else on the floor. He turned off the broom, dropped to his knees and examined the red smudge. Blood. Fresh, not clotted. He noticed a few more drops, and his bones turned into ice. Did the burglar bleed? He did not stop to think that the intruder might still be inside, hiding somewhere. He hurried to the vidisimu to call the abasura.

When the technological revolution started, he had imagined that telephones would become smaller than a thumb. Instead, they ballooned into this twenty-one inch gadget, which also had the functions of the TVs, radios and computers of his childhood. The government issued them for free. He punched a single button, and the screen flashed to life. He pressed another button, which autodialed the emergency number. Rather than the instant connection the old telephone systems were capable of, he would have to wait for two minutes to contact the police.

"Hang up," a woman said, in an accent that stirred memories the Emperor had stifled. For a second he thought he was hallucinating, but he could feel her behind him. He could hear her breathing. He turned around. The sight of her nearly knocked him off his feet. She had shaved off all her hair, and had smeared soot on her body to hide the color of her skin, but her blue eyes and the shape of her nose betrayed her. A mzungu. He did not know that they still existed.

"Please. I don't want to kill you."

He pressed a button, ending the call before a connection could be made.

She had been hiding behind a shelf. He was glad he had not looked there for she might have shot him. She had a flash gun, the kind the abasura used. Strips of bark cloth covered her breasts and loins. Her body was full of wounds and scars. Her presence confirmed that the slave camps still existed. How had she escaped?

She looked young, maybe twenty. Her hands shivered as though from malaria. Her eyes were red, frightened. Tears had made tracks on the soot on her face. Her mouth, a small red thing beneath her long nose, reminded him of what they used to say about white women, that they slept with any man who showed interest. If he asked her, would she accept, even though he had not shaved in four years? His beard grew thick, making him look older than forty. He feared it took away his handsomeness. Long ago, a friend had told him that Wazungu girls preferred smoother chins, which is why their men shaved every day. He wished he had never kept a beard. She reminded him of what was wrong with his marriage. His wife, like every woman he knew, had embraced the Emperor's propaganda that sex for pleasure was not African, that it was the rotten culture of white people, and that it had led to the once incurable disaster, AIDS.

"The key," she said in Kiswahili.

She cannot be real, he thought. He closed his eyes, but when he opened them, she still stood in front of him, her palm thrust out, demanding the key to his ornithopter.

He removed a thin blue pipe from a bunch that hung on a chain around his neck, and gave it to her. He was surprised at how stable his fingers where, for inside he was trembling, his heart beating in chaos, his mind swirling in panic. She snatched the key and sped to the door. He gasped at the wounds on her back, the raw gashes oozing blood, a gift from the whips of the abasura.

Before she could reach the door, a wail of sirens exploded.

"Shit," she said in English.

Kopet followed her gaze out of the window and saw four abasura racing towards the workshop. Sirens flashed on their helmets. Their ornithopters looked like flying unicycles, the wheel and a small engine between their thighs, and three feet long wings attached to their backs. The mzungu could not make a run for it. The abasura had their telephotos on the building. They would recognize her, even from three miles away, and kill her.

"Shit, shit, shit," she said.

He saw the blood slipping down her legs. Before he could give it another thought, he ran to the green shelf and gave it a big shove. It moved easily, revealing a trap door on the floor. He pulled the door open. A rope ladder dropped into a dark hole.

"Get in," he whispered in English, a language he had not spoken in twenty years.

Muttering a million thanks, she vanished into the hole. He pushed the shelf back in place. Quickly, trembling, panicking, he snatched the electric broom and swept away the last bits of glass and the drops of blood.

If the abasura found her, they would shoot him dead. But

again, if they found the things he hid in that hole, they would shoot him dead. He had made the hole fifteen years ago, when the Emperor ordered the abasura to conduct a house-to-house search for items that he said promoted and glorified white people. Books, music, CDs, DVDs, paintings, clothes, anything. Kopet loved his novels - Stephen King, Margaret Atwood, Stieg Larsson; he loved the music of Snow Patrol, J-Lo, Janet Jackson, Damien Rice. He stuffed them all into the hole. The books were still okay. He read them often, but the electronics no longer worked. He could not listen to Missy Elliot or Queen Latifah, not even to Bob Marley's Redemption Song or Tracy Chapman's Talkin' Bout a Revolution. The Emperor claimed such musicians promoted African inferiority because they used white musical instruments and the white language.

The first policeman walked in as the broom wiped off the last drops of blood. Kopet switched off the mop and turned to the soldier.

"I didn't hear you, afande," he said, pointing at the broom. "This thing is so noisy."

The other three soldiers stayed at the door, holding their guns ready.

"We are looking for an escaped slave," the first one said.

"What?" Kopet said. "You mean those white cockroaches are still on our land? NO! I'll squash it under my feet when I see it! Believe me, afande, I'll call you to pick up the corpse!"

They ignored him. They searched his workshop with heat sensors. Kopet held his breath, certain they would detect her, but they did not point their gadgets toward the floor. They did not suspect that he had a secret hole. They pointed them at the ceiling, which was hollow enough to hide a person. He worried about the blood that she must have left behind the shelf where she had hidden, but they did not bother with a visual search of that space. They trusted their heat sensors to detect a person hiding behind the thin plywood. They opened the big boxes with padded surfaces that could mask body heat, and went into the two rooms in the back, but on finding nothing they were satisfied that the fugitive was not in there. Until the broken window caught their attention.

"A bird crashed in yesterday evening," Kopet explained. "I'll fix it today."

They lost interest in the window.

"She is a dangerous woman," the afande who did all the talking said. "She killed one of us and took his gun. When you see her, don't fight. Call us."

They then searched outside the workshop. Kopet feared that they would find the blood trail her wounds must have left, but they found nothing. She had not bled outside. His fears grew as he realized she might suffocate if they stayed too long. She was twelve feet underground in a hole he had built to hide books, not people.

After searching for thirty minutes, they went away. Kopet waited another ten minutes before he let her out. She sucked in air like someone who had been under water for too long.

"Thank you," she said in a subdued whisper.

He nodded. She peered out of the window, searching, but there was no sign of the abasura. She started for the door.

"Stay in," he said. "They are still in the neighborhood. You better wait a few hours." They could not still be in the neighborhood, for there were only two buildings in a radius of five miles, his and the fish factory. He wanted her to stay with him. "You'll be safe in there," he added, pointing toward the back rooms.

"Thank you," she said again. Her lips trembled, as though she wanted to say more, but no words came out.

He led her to the bathroom to clean the soot off her body. After she had washed, he made her lie face down on a bed of papyrus and he smeared herbal medicine on her wounds. It immediately stopped the bleeding. She was red with sunburn. He applied the lotion all over her body, feeling her warmth and the softness of her skin. It had been five years since he last touched a woman. Five years since he last shuddered inside a woman. Desire rushed through his blood, flooding his loins with heat. The temptation nearly overwhelmed him.

He ran out of excuses to touch her. Every inch of her skin was covered in ointment. He sat down on a chair beside the bed. He watched her pretty face, her large eyes.

"Why do you help me?" she said.

Before he could reply, a flapping of wings erupted outside. She stiffened.

"My wife," he said. "She has brought me breakfast. Stay quiet."

He went into the workshop, locking the door behind him. He picked a vase and pretended to wipe dust off it. He knew what she would be wearing even before he saw her - a bra made out of calabashes, a green skirt made out of papyrus fibre, colorful beads on her waist and on her neck, bangles on her arms and ankles. Her hair was braided and bedecked with bright green beads. She had painted her forehead red, to mark her as a married woman, a symbol borrowed from Hindi cultures. She carried the food in a basket, which she put on a table near the door.

"My husband," she said, going down to her knees. "Here is your breakfast."

He did not give her the usual bright smile.

Over the years, his dislike for her had congealed into hatred. They were teenagers when they fell in love. Her name was Akello. He called her Kay. They planned to get married before they turned twenty, but he could not imagine starting a family in the shanty tents of the refugee camp, where they had lived all their lives. They could not go home. It was in ashes after thirty years of war. They wanted to migrate to Europe, or America, or to Australia, somewhere far from the misery, somewhere safe and full of happiness. As luck would have it, out of tens of thousands of applicants, they were chosen to start a new life in Sweden. Their future was set.

But one day, a month before they were to board the plane, they heard a name in the radio, in a strange broadcast from the heart of the chaos their homeland had become. Someone called himself the Emperor. He claimed that, in the space of one month, he had vanquished all the warlords and hundreds of different armed groups. He declared peace and urged all refugees to return home. No one had heard of him before. Nobody believed him. But rumor that he used very powerful juju began to spread. They said his soldiers could fly, that they did not use guns but gadgets that looked like bananas and flashed like a torch. A single flash could kill scores of people. Nobody believed these rumors until scores of winged men flew over the camp in broad daylight.

Magic or not, Kopet and Akello believed their eyes. They dropped the plan to migrate to Sweden and ran hand in hand back to the homeland they had been forced to leave as infants. They found the land magically transformed into a paradise. Its city had buildings that were taller than mountains, five thousand foot high skyscrapers that were built in less than a month. Everybody owned a well furnished three bedroom home. Everybody had a flying machine. Everything was free. They only had to work for food.

How the Emperor had come upon this fantastical technology became a source of great speculation. Most Africans simply put it down to magic, to knowledge from the ancestors. They said that their gods had finally woken up to fight against foreign gods. The Emperor acknowledged these superstitions. He said the gift came through an old man, who never went to school but who was blessed with the ability to design flying machines, modify DNA, blend minerals and chemicals to create new kinds of materials, all to benefit mankind without hurting the environment as the white people had done.

The rich countries in Europe and America did not believe in this superstitious explanation. They believed the Emperor had a secret, and they wanted to know it. They enticed him with money. They sent their smoothest seducers to woo him in feats of diplomacy. They performed every trick in the book, but the Emperor replied with hostility. He hated white people. He blamed them for the misery in Africa, the poverty, the sickness, the famines, the endless wars. He was not willing to share his secret with them. At that time, Kopet and Akello, like every African who had lived a wretched life and now looked forward to a future in paradise, cheered their new leader.

The rich nations then resorted to force. Under the leadership of the USA, the superpowers, China, the European Union, Britain and Russia, joined forces against the Emperor. The CIA claimed he was an agent of a species from outer space, and a threat to human existence. They had to get rid of him. They sent drones to assassinate him, but the aircrafts vanished mysteriously.

They sent thousands of troops with hi-tech fighting gear to the East African coast. They aimed nuclear weapons at the Emperor's territory. "Tell us the secret," they said, "or we smoke you up."

Everyone thought the Emperor would be wiped out. Other than the simple flying machines, which looked like primitive toys from a folktale, and the banana-like flash guns, the Emperor seemed not to have anything to defend himself with. But he defeated the invaders within twenty-four hours. He vaporized their fighter planes and sank an entire fleet of the US Navy in a blink. He wiped out New York City to demonstrate that he possessed something more powerful than nuclear weapons. The invaders threw their hands up in surrender. Africa cheered.

Kopet and Akello had their first child as the drums of victory thundered in the city.

The victory enabled the Emperor to expand his reign to all corners of the continent, and to enslave the people in a new doctrine of hate. He ripped apart the colonial borders. Every tribe regained its identity as a nation of its own. He fuelled a deadly campaign. Africa for Africans. Arabs and Asians were expelled. White people were rounded up and thrown into slave camps. Revenge, the Emperor said. Africans involved in inter-racial relationships were shot dead for betraying their race. As the hate campaigns raged, there cropped up a mad attempt to return to the African way of life before the Europeans came, or to what they believed were authentic African cultures and values.

Akello was swallowed up in the euphoria. She rejected everything non-African. Kopet could no longer recognize the girl he fell in love with, the chubby teenager with four dimples and large eyes that shone like two brilliant moons. She was lost. In her place was this automaton manufactured in a factory of mass hysteria, this strange woman who reduced herself from a lover to a slave.

"Do you remember my name?" he asked her that morning.

She was still on her knees. She looked at him without comprehending his question. He sat on a reed chair, glaring at her, hoping she could see the hatred shinning in his eyes.

"Please, my husband," she said. "Eat your food."

She smiled, showing him perfectly white teeth. She removed the cover from the basket. She had brought him katogo, a mixture of boiled bananas and goat offal, in a clay bowl that he had designed. It could preserve the temperature of food or water for many hours. Beside it was a calabash of milk. He would have preferred tea, the herb of his youth, but that was banned for being non-African. He returned his glare to her.

"You used to call me Mike," he said. "I used to call you Kay."

An angry light flared in her eyes. Over the years, her eyes had acquired a red tint, a result of cooking with firewood. The genetically modified mwiko tree provided an inexhaustible source of fuel, but Kopet never saw the need to use it. Solar stoves did the work more efficiently. His wife, however, preferred open fires in her kitchen. He once asked her why she does not live in a grass hut in the bushes, but he got a tongue lash for being un-African.

"My husband," she said. "How can you think about those colonial names? Does this mean your mind is still enslaved? Should I ask the teacher to visit us this evening?"

He chuckled as if his statement was a joke, but he trembled in sudden fear and he was certain she could see the panic on his face. When he returned home in the evening, he would surely find an old man who would yap into his face all night about why they had to abandon foreign names. Maybe he would end up in jail with hard labor for a couple of days.

"Please leave," he said. "Go back home. I want to eat alone."

The food would have tasted better with a fork, but that too was banned. He had to use his fingers. He touched the food. It scalded his skin.

"But my husband, you know I have to wash your hands after every meal."

"Are you my wife or not?"

"I'm your wife."

"Then you must do as I command."

He saw her hesitation, saw her battling with the indoctrination, which said she should obey her husband, but also said a true African man is not supposed to wash his own hands after a meal. His wife must do that for him.

"You cannot give me that command," she said. "I have to wash your hands after the meal. That is our culture. If I don't, then our ancestors-"

"GO!" he yelled. "Move your ugly ass! Disappear! Go!"

"What have I done to make you angry?"

"GO!"

When she still did not move, he grabbed her by the hair and dragged her out. She squealed in pain. He shoved her out of the door. She fell onto the dirt, bruised her palms and elbow. She looked at him in confusion. Hurt. He ignored her and walked back to the table.

He was about to carry the food to the back room when her shadow fell over the basket. She had returned to the doorway. She did not walk in.

"You hate me," she said.

He recognized the note in her voice. He had heard it only

once before, the day her mother died. He sat down, his back to her, though he very much wanted to look at her face, where he suspected tears were flowing. He felt her eyes burning into his flesh, making him angrier and more nervous.

He forced himself to concentrate on the food. With trembling fingers, he picked a tiny bit of banana and licked it away. He took a tiny sip of the milk. He wanted her to think he was going to eat it. He was hungry, but he planned to give the food to the fugitive, she needed it more. Akello stood at the doorway for nearly ten minutes before he heard her walking away. Only then did he look up. Through the window he saw her bruka leap into the air. He waited until she had vanished before taking the food to the fugitive.

Indeed, the slave was starving. He watched her devour the meal with her bare hands, in a savage fashion, smearing her mouth with grease from the goat offal. She gulped down the milk, and some of it splashed onto her chin. The sound of her feasting accentuated the silence. When she had licked every bit off the bowl, drained the gourd of the milk, she lay on the bed, facedown, and promptly fell asleep.

He threw a light bed sheet made out of bark over her. After about five minutes of admiring her and fantasying about what a great time he would have once her wounds healed, he went back into the workshop to paint flowers on a vase. He remembered the gift he had given Akello on the day he had asked her to marry him, a vase. It had a circular pattern of yellow and blue, her favorite colors. That vase still survived. She kept it in their living room. He often thought that she had stuffed their love into it the way people used to put ashes of the dead in urns, as though it were something to be admired from afar, a reminder of what they once had and can never enjoy again.

Akello certainly would report his behavior, tell the abasura how he had used colonial names and that he had stopped her from performing her duties. The abasura would then throw him in jail for several days of hard labor, and subject him to the torturous sermon of a cultural teacher every evening. They would try to make him behave like everyone else, to pretend that his first twenty years never existed, that he never went to school to get an education modeled on non-African values, to abandon love and romance in the name of the reintroduction of African culture. He could not take that kind of life anymore.

He looked at the vase he was painting, at the flowers, and he had the sudden dream of dropping everything and running away with the mzungu. Fleeing somewhere far out of sight, far from the hate. They could make a paradise of their own in a little island of seclusion. But where would such a place be? Would she agree to it simply because he had saved her life?

He became aware of the dim image of his face caught in the vase, his eyes looking vacant, his beard thick on his face. Would she find him attractive? He ran into the bathroom, rummaged through the shelves until he found an old razor, and then he slashed off his beard. He cut himself a few times. In a few days bumps would form all over his chin, but he liked the fresh image he saw. The beauty of his youth once again graced his smile. He was glad to see that the dimples of his childhood were still deep and enchanting.

He peeped at the sleeping woman. She snored lightly, her eyes closed in deep peace. The medicine he had rubbed on her body had stained the bed sheets. It gave the room a faint, sweetish odor that made him think of flowers in the paradise he would create with her. Quietly, he closed the door and hurried to the vidisimu.

He punched the machine into life, called up a map and searched for paradise. He found it after two hours. A tiny island about three hundred meters in diameter, hidden away in a vast swamp in the Kyoga basin. The nearest neighbor would be ten miles away. The seller suggested it would be a nice spot for a fish farm. The price was half of his monthly earnings. A bird's eye video showed a natural fountain in the island, sprouting into a small stream that sparkled in the sunlight as it flowed through the lush greenery into the swamp. Little trees with brightly colored flowers grew all around. Birds sang and insects chirped happily. He could see himself on a canoe, fishing in the stream, while his mzungu swam stark naked, her hair floating in the water like a separate living creature.

Before the dream could fade into doubt and reason, he paid for the island and instantly received the land title. He printed out the documents of the transaction, as well as a map and video image of the island, and then he shut down the vidisimu. He laid the video print on the table, and watched the one-minute segment play itself over and over again.

"What are you smiling at?"

The voice startled him out of his reverie. She had woken up. She walked over to the table, her footsteps so light that she made no sound as she glided over the wooden floor. She looked at the video, and then turned to him, a question in her eyes.

"I just bought it," he said. "For you."

Her eyes widened. She looked at the video again, and then at his smiling face. He hoped she could see he had shaved for her.

"There is no neighbor for ten miles," he said. "You could live there forever and no one would ever find you. But, of course, you won't be alone." He paused for effect. His smile showed off a strong set of teeth and black gums, a smile his wife had once described as 'dashing.' "I'll be with you."

She collapsed onto a chair and buried her face in her palms. He hated himself for being so blunt, but he could not think of anything else he could have said to her. How else could he seduce her in such a short time? In the novels and films he used to enjoy, the hero had to woo the heroine with flowers and dinner dates. They had to get to know each other well before falling madly in love and living happily ever after. He did not have the luxury of time to engage in that kind of romance. He pictured himself to be in a story in which the heroic deed of the boy helps him win the girl without going through the phase of flowers and dining. He had saved her life. What could be more heroic than that?

"My mother said she once had a black lover," she finally spoke, looking up at him. Her small mouth trembled, and he thought it was with an urge to kiss him. "I didn't believe her. I thought all blacks were evil. But now I see what she meant when she said there are good black people."

She paused. Their eyes locked. A green cloud of light blossomed from her eyes. His heart revved up in anticipation. It was going to be as easy as he had imagined.

"But tell me," she said. "What happens if two years down the road someone sets up a home near the island? What happens if a bruka flies by and someone sees a white woman playing amidst the flowers?"

Kopet had not thought about that. The happily ever after of his dreams had seemed so real that there could not be a bleak possibility. He looked down at the video print again, saw the birds flying in an endless loop, the butterflies hovering over the flowers, the fountain shooting water into the sky, the stream sparkling in the sunlight.

"I don't want to be a fugitive for the rest of my life," she said. "I was born in a camp. I've lived there all my life. But I refuse to be a slave anymore. I want freedom."

He wanted to sit down beside her and throw his arms around her. He wanted to tell her that she would not be his slave, and that he would do everything in his power to see that she lives the rest of her life in paradise.

"I was flying to Europe when the bruka crashed," she said. "It was an old model. It could not endure a non-stop long distance flight, especially with the abasura chasing me. But it was the only thing I could steal from the camp." She looked out of the door, at his yellow aircraft gleaming in the sunshine. "Yours has an engine. What speed can it do? Three hundred?"

He nodded, still unable to speak.

"Mum said that Europe is about six thousand kilometers away. That means I can make it in - how many hours? Eighteen? Twenty? Twenty four?"

No one Kopet knew had attempted that kind of journey on the small aircraft. Maybe it could survive a day of non-stop flight. Maybe not.

"You could come with me," she said. "I hear Europe is a better place."

That's what he heard a lifetime ago, when still in the refugee camps. He wondered what kind of life he would have had if he and Akello had gone to Sweden. He wondered even more whether he would be happier if he eloped with this mzungu. Such a flight would be futile. His wife would notice his absence sooner or later. She would then call the abasura, who would scan the air and pick out his bruka from the hundreds of millions.

Even if they somehow made it, he could not be sure that Europe was a better place, especially not for him. For ten years the Emperor had closed Africa to the world, arguing that such a blackout would ensure a proper re-indoctrination of his people. No news came in. No news went out. The last news from outside was grim. Nazis and the Ku Klux Klan had re-emerged. Millions of blacks were expelled from Europe and America, those who refused to leave were lynched and enslaved.

"I cannot stay here," she said. "I have to go."

He nodded. There was no way for them to be together. No fairytale romance. No paradise. Just a dream of what it might have been if the world was a better place.

"It is impossible to escape," she said. "But I'll die trying."

It hurt that his dreams were simply that, childish dreams. He avoided looking at her, as though that would bring back the happiness he derived from his fantasies just a few minutes ago. He was aware of her physical presence, of her warmth. He remembered the feel of her skin on his fingers. She exuded a pleasant scent, like a mixture of onions and lemons, courtesy of the herbal ointment he had smeared on her.

"If you set off now, you might just be able to make it." He spoke in a voice so low he could barely hear himself. "Two solar blocks power the engine, but I suggest you do more peddling during the day so as to ensure you don't run out of power in the night."

She seemed surprised by the offer. She slowly rose to her feet and touched his shoulder. Her palms were warm. She kissed his cheek. Her lips were warm. Then she kissed him on the lips, a long kiss that left him breathless. She broke away, they looked into each other's eyes for several seconds, and he saw a light sparkling in her eyes, a vision of what happiness means. She suddenly turned away from him and ran out.

He followed her to the door, and watched her climb into the bruka. The windows were tinted, to reduce the amount of sunlight getting into the aircraft. This worked to her advantage. A casual observer would not notice a hairless white woman piloting the craft. He saw her examine the controls for several seconds. Though his was the latest model, the controls were very similar to that of the first models. She would have no problem learning to fly it on the go.

He stood on the door watching the sky long after she had vanished into the blue. Only then did he realize that he did not know her name.

What he did next, how he explained his missing bruka, could help her escape or destroy her. First, he fixed the broken window. Next, he closed the door and all the windows, drawing the curtains. Anyone who came to the workshop would think there was no one home. To cement the illusion, he called home. He was relieved that their eldest child, and not Akello, answered.

"I've just bought land to start a fish farm," he told the boy. "Please tell your mother that I will be out all day. I won't return home until late in the night, maybe until after midnight."

"Okay," the boy said.

He shut down the vidisimu. He stood for several moments watching it, expecting it to flash into life with a call from his wife, who would demand that she serves him lunch first as was her duty. The machine stayed dead.

He went down into his secret hole. He found a rosary on the wall. The mzungu woman had left it behind, a farewell gift.

Though he had not been a Catholic, he wore it. The warm wood embraced his skin with memories of her kiss.

She floated in his head as he searched through the pile of musty books. When he came upon Fried Green Tomatoes at the Whistle Stop Café, memories of Akello flooded in, filling him with confusing emotions. He pulled the book from the pile. Puffs of dust stung his nose as he flipped through the pages. He could not remember why the book had caught his attention, that day a lifetime ago in the refugee camp. He had attempted to steal it from the library. Being the only copy, it was in the reference only section. The librarian caught him, and banned him from using the library for a month. Several days later, Akello surprised him when she ran into his tent, waving the book. She had succeeded in stealing it.

Now, he took it to the backroom and lay on the bed. The warmth of the fugitive was still on the sheets, the sweetish scent of onions and lemons still lingered in the air, the dreams that she ignited still burned in his brain. A heavy cloud enshrouded him, as it dawned that he could never find another love like Akello. His sweet Kay was now lost to him.

He began to read. The words of Flagg transported him back to the lost world, where blacks were the oppressed. He did not know if that was a better world, but he wished to go back to it, if only to once again swim in the love of Kay.

Night came. Darkness filled the room. He wondered how far the mzungu had gone, whether she was still free and flying to freedom, or whether they had intercepted her and she was now in a torture chamber somewhere, chained, or back in a slave camp. There would be no mention of her in the news. The Emperor wanted to erase white people from memory. He decreed that talking about them, for whatever reason, was a capital crime. Kopet recalled a neighbor who, while supping with his family, had talked about a German friend he once had. The man's six-year-old son had then asked, 'What is a mzungu?' and the man's wife had quickly replied, 'It's an imaginary creature like the flying pigs'. The next day she reported him to the abasura and they executed him at the firing squad.

Kopet switched on a small lamp, shielded the light and continued reading. When the vidisimu rang, he jumped up on the bed in fright. It was nearly nine o'clock. He was supposed to be home. He turned off the light and sat tense on the bed until the vidisimu went quiet. It erupted again several minutes later. He listened to the bells peal for long time before the caller gave up. For the next hour, there were ten other calls, then a long silence. He wondered when Akello would report his absence to the abasura. When they would scan the skies for his aircraft, trace it within an hour and force it to land. He closed his eyes and prayed for the fugitive.

They had destroyed all churches and mosques, all Hindu temples and the magnificent Bahai temple that once stood on a hill in Kampala. Yet they could not take away his faith. Sometimes he thought of the Emperor as the antichrist in the book of Revelations. Now, he fingered the rosary the fugitive had left behind, as he had seen Catholics do, and said a prayer for her protection.

The flapping of wings interrupted his prayer. A bruka shone a light upon the workshop. He sighed, relieved that it was not a police search. It must be Akello. The thought gave him hope. She had not yet reported his absence. The fugitive still had a chance. The bruka hovered about for nearly ten minutes before going away.

He could not read anymore. He was afraid to turn on the lights. He could not pray. He was afraid to breath, thinking that someone would hear and know he was hiding in the darkness. He sat still, listening to the music of crickets, to an owl on the roof. He fell asleep.

He only meant to close his eyes for a few moments and then call his wife at midnight. When he opened them, daylight filled the room. Hunger tickled his stomach. The thought that he had overslept and ruined the mzungu's escape banged his head like a hammer. If he had called home at midnight, he might have cooked up a story that his wife would have believed. Now, she would be certain that something had happened to him. She probably had already reported it to the abasura, and they had probably already scanned the skies and found the fugitive. He staggered into the workshop, running for the vidisimu, hoping it had not happened as he feared, that the mzungu still had a chance.

He punched a button to start the vidisimu, and then he heard a voice that filled him with a sense of déjà vu.

"Hello, Mike," a woman said.

It struck him as though someone had fired a freezer gun and turned him into a block of ice. A ghost. The ghost of Kay. No one ever called him Mike. They used to call him Michael. But it could not be a ghost. The Kay he knew and loved no longer existed. She had transformed into Akello, a creature obsessed with the Emperor's insane indoctrination. Yet it could not be Akello. It had to be Kay. The ghost from the past. She had floated through time and spoken in a voice that tinkled in the murky light of dawn like the song of a clock. She had called him Mike.

Slowly, he turned around. A figure sat in the shadows. It

wore a flowered yellow dress. He remembered that dress. He had bought it for her on her eighteenth birthday, with the first money he earned as a potter. He was now certain she was a ghost for he had watched that dress burn in a bonfire against white culture. Akello must have died in the night and now her ghost had came to haunt him.

"I remember your name," she said. "I remember this dress."

She stood up, and then he realized the dress was not made of cotton, but of paper. It was an imitation of the gift. His terror turned into confusion. She walked towards him, the dress rustling. The movement caused it to rip, and fall off her body. She had nothing on underneath. Her breasts pointed at him like mangoes. She threw her arms around him and kissed him in the mouth, the way she had first kissed him in the camp. They had been in a classroom, at night, revising their books, no other student in sight, when suddenly the lights went out in a power blackout. The moon shone through the windows, painting a magical blue world. Without a word, she walked over to his desk and kissed him, starting their romance. Two months later, he bought her that dress. Now, she kissed him again with the same passion of newfound love. He tasted her tongue, after such a long time, bit into her luscious lips, felt her breasts pressing hard against him, felt her warmth flood into his blood.

They made love on the wooden floor. He enjoyed once again listening to her groans and the sounds of pleasure that had graced his tent. He whispered into her ears, the same promises he made to her ages ago. He told her how much he still loved her. She replied in whispers and soft moans, asking him to forgive her for betraying their love, reassuring him that she still loved him. They came at the same time, the world exploding, and for a minute they lay on the floor, shuddering in the aftermath of orgasm, entangled in each other's limbs, smeared in each other's fluids.

He stared at the ceiling, at the murals he had painted after the old man died, at the yellow birds and red flowers in a green field. He heard her breathing slow down, felt her fingers playing with the hair on his chest, and her words flowed into his ears like a fresh stream feeding a draught stricken land.

"I don't want you to hate me," she said.

He did not reply. He thought about the love they had just made. For a moment he feared she merely wanted another baby. But while they made the last two children, she had merely lain stiff on the bed, her thoughts on the Emperor's vision, as he pounded away. This morning had been different. She had resurrected something that he had imagined was long dead and buried.

"When you didn't come home last night," she continued, "I wanted to call the abasura. I knew you were hiding from me. But I knew if I did I would lose you forever. I came back after midnight and found you asleep. I saw the book in your hand. I remembered what we had before. The happiness."

He wiped off the tears that rolled down her cheeks and slipped onto the wooden floor.

"Please forgive me," she said. "I want to heal what I destroyed."

He thought it was all a dream. He did not want it to end. He kissed her, and again they made love. They lay shuddering in each other's arms for the next hour, not saying anything.

"I have a surprise for you," he finally broke the silence.

He showed her the video print of the island. He painted a picture of a little hut, of her swimming in the stream, he fishing on a canoe. Their children were all grown up. Soon, they would start homes of their own. Then, he and Akello could migrate to the little island, where they could live in relative isolation, far away from the madness of the Emperor.

"Will you live there with me?" he said.

"I'll do anything for you," she said.

He did not tell her about the fugitive. Instead, he waited until the afternoon, when he was sure twenty four hours had passed, enough time for the mzungu to reach Europe, before he reported the loss of his bruka. They scanned the air, but found no trace of it. Three days later the police had not found the aircraft. Then he knew that the fugitive had made it safely. If they had found her, they would have arrested him for aiding her escape.

He thanked God for hearing his prayers, and he thanked the fugitive for coming into his life. In a strange way, she had helped to heal his marriage, helped to make his wife realize where true happiness lay. ✷

The Yellow People

The storm fell from a blue sky. It started as a playful drizzle, with the sun still shinning, and then daylight went out and bucketfuls of water slammed against the glass doors of the supermarket, imprisoning Tom Dunningan and several other people in the shop. The shop, originally intended for a small retail business, had only two aisles. The shelves were so crammed that some goods had to be placed on the floor. The Indian owner, Kapoor, sat behind the counter beside the door, frequently scanning the security mirrors in the ceiling. His assistant, a woman in her twenties, sat on a stool at the extreme end of the room. The five shoppers were crowded near the door, clutching plastic bags, waiting for the rain to stop. Dunningan was deep inside the supermarket though he too had finished shopping. He stared at an old man with no thumbs. He had always believed he was fearless, since he was the grim reaper's helper, but the sight of this old man had unnerved him. His face had wrinkled such that he looked eighty, rather than fifty. His beard, which he usually kept neatly trimmed, looked like wet feathers. After a decade living in Uganda, he had acquired a deep tan, but the moment he noticed that this old man had no thumbs, his skin had turned white as if smeared with flour. His knees trembled. Dizziness made him sway. He leaned against a shelf for support.

"Give him a seat," Kapoor said to the assistant. He had to shout to be heard above the roar of the rain.

Dunningan forced a smile in thanks. He was used to such privileges. As a white man living in a small African town, he got a lot of attention. He liked to think it was because he started the school for poor children, and not because of his skin color.

Without a word, the assistant offered him her stool. He collapsed onto it and closed his eyes. Maybe it is just a bad dream, he thought. Maybe I'm just imagining that it is the same old man, and that he has no thumbs.

"Are you fine?"

He opened his eyes. Kapoor now stood beside him. Unlike most Indians he had met in the country, Kapoor spoke fluent English without an accent. Dunningan held his breath to calm his heart. He forced a smile at Kapoor, but it ended up a grimace.

"I could give you a bed in the back room to rest," Kapoor said.

"I'm okay," Dunningan said. His lips quivered. His voice crackled like dry twigs.

"You don't look okay," Kapoor said. "What's the matter?"

Dunningan's eyes automatically returned to the old man, who clutched a shopping bag full of insecticide tins. The man had attained a darker hue, as though he had smeared himself with charcoal dust. He wore an outlandish bright yellow costume made from fine silk. It looked like long sleeved coveralls which fit so tightly that Dunningan could see every curve on the scrawny body. His shoes looked like yellow stockings with wooden soles. He starkly contrasted with the ordinary looking jeans, t-shirts, kitenges, coats and ties the other people wore. He had no hair. His head shone in the fluorescent lights. The last time Dunningan had seen him, two months ago, he had been entombed in the backyard crypt. What then was he doing among the living in a supermarket?

"Do you see him?" Dunningan whispered.

Kapoor dropped, putting his ears closer to Dunningan's mouth. "What?"

"Him." Dunningan's voice was hoarse and weak. "That yellow

man."

"Him? He is a very weird fellow," the Indian said, and Dunningan's bones melted into a cold liquid. The old man was not a ghost. "I first saw him two weeks ago," Kapoor added.

"Two weeks?" Dunningan said. The pallor of his face deepened. When he had visited the tomb three days before, to put in a new corpse, nothing seemed amiss.

"Tom," Kapoor said. "You need to see a doctor."

"I'm fine," Dunningan snapped. "Just tell me about him."

"You are sick," Kapoor said. "Come, let's go get you a warm bed."

Dunningan felt cold fingers on his shoulder. He jumped, slapping them away. And then he saw it was only Kapoor. He smiled to hide his shame.

"I'm sorry," Dunningan said. "I'm a little – Look, I'll go to the clinic the moment it stops raining, but I need to know about that man."

"Why?" Dunningan could not answer. He could not tell the Indian about the tomb in his backyard. "Do you know him?" Kapoor added.

Dunningan made it a point not to know the identity of his victims, but he could not forget their faces. He, especially, could not forget that of this old man, the third elderly person he had killed in his career. The first two had been his parents.

"Yes," Dunningan finally said, finding a plausible answer. "He wants a place for his child at the school. I'm still reviewing his application. I wonder if I should accept it. Tell me what you know about him. I think he is rich yet the scholarships are only for poor children."

"Well," Kapoor said. "I don't know much about him really.

He often comes with a woman who wears the same clothes and also doesn't have thumbs. I think they are twins. They don't look alike, but they have exactly the same voice."

A wave of dizziness nearly threw Dunningan off the seat. There were two escapees from the crypt in his backyard, two of the three hundred and seventy people he had killed and entombed. He bit his lip to stifle the shock.

"Where is she?" he asked.

"She didn't come today," Kapoor said. "Tom, you need to lie down. Come, let me give you a bed."

He again touched Dunningan's shoulder, but Dunningan shoved him off.

"What do they buy?" Dunningan said.

"Insecticide. Tom – "

"Insecticide?"

"Yeah," Kapoor said. "It's very strange. They always buy a dozen tins each time, and they come twice a week. What do they need all that for? When I asked, they said the doctor sends them for it."

"Doctor?"

"I don't understand either, but it's good business for me. I don't ask questions."

Outside, the rain relented to a harsh drizzle. The tree in front of the shop groaned in the fury of the shrill wind. The shoppers still could not leave the supermarket.

"Well," Kapoor said, after a silence had cropped up between them. "You go straight to the clinic after the rain, okay?"

"Okay."

Dunningan closed his eyes again, and tried to think about the school, hoping it would distract him from the old man. There had to be a rational explanation, he thought. Maybe he had put these two in the crypt when they were still alive. But where did they get that costume? Who was this doctor? Why did he send them for a lot of insecticide?

#

The moment the rain stopped, the old man and the other shoppers dashed out. Dunningan ran after him. The street was littered with debris from the storm. Leaves, broken branches, upturned trash cans. Water filled the potholes. Children raced paper boats in the gutters. Clouds hung low above the old buildings, sweeping fast over the rust colored roofs. The old man had a brisk gait. His footsteps seemed to echo all over the town as he splashed across the pavement. Dunningan overtook him and stood in front of him, forcing him to stop.

"I greet you," Dunningan said in Adhola. When he had just come to Tororo town, he took trouble to learn the language of the locals. He became fluent within three months.

The old man's eyes were white, like a baby's, the pupils a deep black. They did not reflect light, they were just two black and white balls in his face. He had a scar on his neck, barely visible under the collar. Dunningan had made it as he throttled him to death.

"Hell-o. To. You. Too," the old man said. He did not stutter, but he put long pauses between the syllables. His voice was hollow, as though he were speaking from inside a pipe. As he spoke, the wrinkles on his face moved as though worms were crawling under his skin.

"So we meet again," Dunningan said.

The old man shook his head. "So – rry," he said, smiling. "I. Lost. Mem – mo – ry."

Dunningan did not realise he was holding his breath until that moment. His chest relaxed. He felt something wash through his veins and he knew it was relief. At least this man had not come back from the dead with vengeance.

"So you don't remember me?" he said.

The old man shook his head again

"What happened to your voice? You spoke properly the last time we talked."

"I. Don't. Know," the old man said.

"What do you do with the insecticide?"

"Doc - tor."

"Who is this doctor?"

"I. Don't. Know."

"What does he use the insecticide for?"

"I. Don't. Know."

A bodaboda came riding down the street. The old man walked closer to the road and raised his arm to stop the bicycle taxi.

"Let me give you a lift," Dunningan said.

If he knew where the old man went, he might unravel the mystery. He had to know why this man had returned to the world of the living. He did not expect the old man to agree, but the old man gave him a shy smile and, without waiting for another word, walked to his car. There were three vehicles in the street, but the old man picked out the right car without being told.

How did he know my car? Dunningan wondered.

When he had picked up the old man, late one night in Naluwerere slum, he had been driving a Mark II that he had rented from Kampala city, and he had applied special effects make-up to look African. He had killed the old man in the backseat of that Mark II. There was no reason why this man should know that this Land Cruiser was his, yet he did. Had Dunningan made a mistake somewhere?

Had the old man really lost his memory?

The old man climbed into the passenger seat, placed his shopping bag on his lap, and again gave Dunningan a smile. This time, his lips parted and Dunningan realized he had no front teeth. He hesitated to enter the car. Something deadly was afoot, something that resurrected corpses and dressed them up in costumes of fine silk. Whatever it was, he had to face it sooner or later. He jumped behind the wheel.

"Where do I take you?" he said, as he fired up the engine.

The old man did not reply at once. A smile wavered on his face as he watched the wipers cleaning the windscreen.

"Headmaster!" Kapoor's assistant ran out of the supermarket waving a shopping bag. "You forgot your things."

"Many thanks," Dunningan said. He rolled down a window and she put the bag on the back seat. After she had gone, Dunningan turned back to the zombie. "Where do we go?"

The old man directed him to the foot of a little mountain, a green volcanic plug that towered above the sleepy town, giving it a postcard facade. The residents called it 'the rock'. They drove by a golf course, and then off the road into a small, overgrown path, which eventually petered out. They abandoned the car and wadded through thick undergrowth. The trees grew thicker and taller as they went higher up the rock, until they were in a jungle. Monkeys watched them. Insects pecked at Dunningan. He could hear the roar of heavy trucks on the highway.

"Where are you taking me?" he asked.

"Home," the old man said.

"You need a lot of Doom to kill mosquitoes here."

"We. Don't. Use. It. For. Mos - quit - O."

Halfway up the mountain, the old man stopped beside a huge boulder. It had a hole near the base. The old man pushed his hand into the hole, pulled something, and part of the stone's surface moved to reveal the mouth of a tunnel. Yellow light spilled out of the hole. He went down on his knees and crawled in. Dunningan hesitated, took a deep breath, and then followed.

The tunnel led to a cave that looked like a honeycomb. Here, the yellow light looked like smoke. It came from egg-like objects on the floor, which was covered with a silky rug. A sweet perfume made Dunningan dizzy. The old man vanished into one of the cells. Dunningan touched the wall. It was spongy, and warm. It stained his finger with a yellowish, gooey substance. A woman crept out of another cell. She too wore a yellow outfit and she had no thumbs. He had kidnapped her in Kigali, a day's drive away. He had entombed her four weeks before he throttled the old man.

"I know you too," he said, in French.

"I don't know that language," the woman said, in Adhola. Her voice was exactly like that of the old man, as though it were the same person speaking through different mouths. She, however, was more fluent in her speech.

"You spoke French," Dunningan said.

The woman gave him a smile, and shook her head. "I only know Adhola."

"Where do you come from?"

She shrugged. "I don't know."

"I found you in Kigali."

"Really?" Her smile vanished. "Where is that?"

"It was your home," he said.

"No," she said. "My home is here." Then, after a moment's

consideration, she added, “Maybe you are right. I lost my memory. I’ll ask the doctor.”

“Is he in?”

“No.”

“Where is he?”

“He comes at midnight.”

Four more people crept out of the cells. They all had no thumbs. They all wore silky yellow clothing and shoes with wooden soles. They all used to be the lifeless residents of his charnel house. It only took him a moment to place each face - where he had picked each up, how he had killed them. Yet here they were, in this surreal cave, smiling at him, their teeth gleaming in the yellow light.

He quickly searched through the cells. They were bare. He did not even see the shopping bags of insecticide. He examined the walls for hollow spots where they might hide things, but did not find any. It was not a very big cave. It had a diameter of about sixty feet. The roof, he now noticed, was swathe in what looked like yellow cobwebs. No spiders were visible.

He went back to the first cell. The thumbless people were all smiling at him. He touched the woman’s hand, and felt for her pulse. Nothing. Without asking, he took a knife out of his pocket and slashed off her left pinky finger. She did not cry out in pain. She did not bleed. She only smiled at him. The finger twitched in his palm, like a maggot. He dropped it.

She held up her hand, to show him another pinky finger growing to replace the one he had cut off. Then, she picked the finger from the floor and put it in his coat pocket.

“Keep it,” she whispered into his ears. “The doctor will come to you this night. He’ll answer your questions. Please, go now.”

She shoved him toward the exit.

#

Dunningan thought work might distract him from what had to be a bad dream. He went to the school. It was five o'clock. Teachers milled about preparing to go home. Students retreated to the dormitories having survived another day of classes. When he got into his office, the shock set in.

He tried to light a cigarette. He could not hold the lighter and did not notice that he had the wrong end of the cigarette in his mouth. He did not realize he was crying until a tear drop fell on the cigarette. He had last cried when he was twelve, the night he had killed his parents. They had refused to buy him an Iron Man toy. He used a fireman's axe, which his father had bought from WalMart earlier in the day. He waited until supper time. He pulled the axe from under the dining table and split his father's skull open. His mother had fainted. He hacked off her head in three blows. Then, to convince the police of his innocence, he had hacked at his own leg, breaking bones, to make it look like an intruder had done the killing.

Now, he dried his eyes. Unable to contain the emotions running riot in his chest, he ran out of the office. He jumped into his car, fired up the engine, reversed and crashed into the administration building. Teachers ran out of the staff room, and stared. He ignored them. He drove to the gate. The Land Cruiser wobbled like a drunk zigzagging home. He swerved off the road and rammed into a tree. Cursing, he got out, kicked the truck, and walked home.

He lived alone in a mansion behind the school, five miles away from town, from the yellow cave that zombies called home. He had lived alone since he turned twenty, after killing his foster father, a distant uncle who refused to give him a loan to start an online dating site insisting he goes to college. This time, Dunningan had made him drunk, and then staged a suicide.

He had then moved from Washington, in the USA, to California. His dating site became successful, earning him millions of dollars. He fell in love with a woman, but he ended up killing her in an accident. He kept her thumbs, for reasons he could not fathom. He did not understand what happened next, how he ended up the person the press called Mr. Thumbs, for he had no intention of becoming a serial killer. After five years, with twelve thumbless corpses all over California, he feared the police would catch him. They had sophisticated crime scene investigation techniques. He would slip up, leaving just a trace of DNA, and then he would spend the rest of his life in jail.

He read about countries with very weak police forces, with such high levels of corruption that he believed he could kill a person a day and no one would notice. If they did, he could easily pay his way out of trouble. Being a white person with a lot of money, they would give him the power and privilege.

He sold off his dating site and relocated to Uganda with two hundred and fifty million US dollars to spend on charity. The government gave him part of a forest to build the school. He settled in, and resumed killing. He had to be very careful this time. If a thumbless corpse showed up, the police in the USA would figure out he was Mr. Thumbs. So he constructed a secret tomb under his mansion. After ten years, he had come to love his life. His money steadily accumulated in several banks, funding his school project, which in turn gave him the perfect cover. In California, he had learnt special effects make-up, so he could become an African anytime he wanted to. He loved his life. It was perfect, until he walked into Kapoor's shop and saw one of his thumbless corpses. Alive.

Dunningan collapsed onto a sofa, with a bottle of whiskey in his hand. He drank long swigs. Something twitched in his pocket. The Kigali woman's finger. He fished it out. Four veins protruded from it like tentacles. They twitched this way and that way, searching. One vein found his wrists and attached itself on his skin. The other three immediately shot out and sank into his flesh. Pain. The veins turned red as blood gushed into the finger.

He yelped and tore the finger off his wrist. Blood spattered. He threw it onto the floor, where it wriggled, the tentacles shooting this way and that way, searching. For him. He ran into the bathroom and bandaged his wrist to stop the bleeding.

He returned to the living room with a garden fork, pricked the finger in one prong, and took it down into the basement, where a thirteen year old boy lay in the darkness, chained to the wall, starving to death. Dunningan had kidnapped him from River Road in Nairobi. The kid had already survived five days without food or water and looked set to live forever. Dunningan threw the finger at him. The tentacles stabbed the boy's neck. Blood spurt out, but for only a brief spell. Soon, the bleeding stopped. The boy twitched, and then went still. Dead.

The finger continued to twitch, wriggling, snaking its way into the boy's neck, until it vanished, leaving a hole in the neck.

"Hello Tom," a voice said. The old man's voice. The Kigali's woman's voice. The hollow voice.

Dunningan jumped and fell against the wall. He turned to see a tall man in the yellow outfit. Dunningan had picked him up in Soroti town, over a hundred kilometers away, and drowned him in a bathtub eight years ago, but the man showed no sign of decomposition.

"Did I scare you?" the man said. He spoke in Adhola, just like the old man and the Kigali woman. "I'm the doctor."

Dunningan pressed himself against the wall, struggling to regain control of his nerves, to not let his fear show. He held his breath, to slow down the beating of his heart. He bit his lips, to stop them from trembling.

The doctor squatted beside the boy. He put his finger on the hole in the neck, and then he turned back to Dunningan with a broad smile.

"In twelve days, the boy will wake up, and he'll walk again. Do you want to cut off his thumbs now?"

Dunningan swallowed. A salty lump was stuck in his throat. It could not be zombies, he thought. A mysterious creature was taking over dead bodies.

"You are right," the man said. "We call it endosymbiosis."

Dunningan wondered if he had spoken out aloud.

"No, you didn't," the man said, with a smile. "We can read your mind."

He put out a hand to help Dunningan to his feet, but Dunningan only stared at the stump where his thumb had been.

"You have many questions," the doctor said. "Let's go down to your tomb. I'll give you the answers."

The doctor carried the dead boy and went back up the steps without waiting for a response. Dunningan sat still until the man had vanished, until he heard the distant sound of the back door opening and closing, and then he followed. The moon stood full and bright. A chilly breeze swept the early night, making the mango tree tremble. Under this tree was a small house in which he kept an emergency generator. It also hid the door to the tomb.

He peeled off a stone slab, revealing a trap door. He went through it, down a wooden ladder, into a chamber he called The Thumb Room. Hundreds of thumbs, of all sizes, shapes, and colors, were mummified, and displayed on the tables, on the walls, and on the ceiling. He went through another door into the tomb. The doctor had lit a dozen hurricane lamps, which were suspended on a row of poles in the middle of the crypt. It was a long room. The wooden walls bore hundreds of pigeonholes in which he kept corpses in sacks. Nothing seemed amiss. However, when he checked one sack, he found a dummy inside. It explained why he had never discovered the missing corpses before. Once he sacked a body and shoved it into a pigeonhole, he never checked it again.

About midway inside the room, the yellow light he had seen in the cave flowed out of a cubicle. He walked to it, and found it empty. No sack. No dummy. Instead, it opened into a tunnel. He climbed in. It was just big enough for him to crawl on his stomach. It sloped deep into the bowels of the earth, and then opened into another honeycomb, much larger than the cave.

In the nearest cell, the recently dead boy and ten thumbless corpses lay on wooden slabs. There were dozens of used insecticide tins under the slabs. On a shelf above the corpses, there were creatures that looked like octopi in transparent stone jars filled with water. Their tentacles twitched and twisted.

The doctor emerged from one of the cells. "There you are," he said.

"Who are you?" Dunningan said. His voice crackled like dry twigs.

"Dead people," the man said, laughing, showing off his thumbless hands. The laughter sounded like a series of car honks. "Sorry," he added. "Just a joke. You humans like to laugh. It is something we don't do in our world."

The man turned around and walked back into the cell he had come from.

"Follow me," he said, as he vanished.

Dunningan followed him. His feet sank into the rug as though he were walking on mud. The perfume made his nose drip. They went through a labyrinth, passing more corpses on slabs, with the tiny octopi hanging above the bodies, and tins of insecticide underneath, until they came to a stone wall. It was smooth and circular. Yellow light, but a darker shade than what he had seen, flowed from behind it. The doctor pushed against the wall. It moved, revealing a room full of giant octopi, and more dead humans on the floor. A hollow hissing sound filled the room.

"This is our –" he paused, searching for the words, and then said in English, "spacecraft." He continued in Adhola. "Is that the word in your language?

"We crashed into this world a few thousand of your years ago and have been marooned here ever since. We, at first, interacted with the humans we found here. We learnt their language and they tried to help us. But we ran out of our food. We couldn't eat anything in this world. We could not repair our ship. We lost all hope. We went into hibernation. The years passed. Our ship sank into the ground and a forest grew over it. Then, you built that tomb right next to us. For the first time we came into contact with dead humans. I discovered that we can inhabit a dead body and be able to live properly in this world. Endosymbiosis. In this case, it involves combining a living creature and a dead one. It was not easy. We kept experimenting until a few months ago, when I found out how to do it perfectly and easily with insecticide." He smiled again. "We had to steal money from your safe to buy it.

Sorry. Now we can feed, and procreate. We'll make this our home until we fix our ship."

The doctor pulled the door closed, shutting out the incessant hollow hiss. Dunningan looked into his eyes for a long moment, eyes that remained dead white and black even in the bright yellowness.

"What arc you going to do about us now?" the doctor asked.

Dunningan did not have an answer. The events had unfolded at such a pace that he had not thought about it. He had feared that zombies walking about might lead to his discovery, but now he did not know if the aliens were a blessing. He could keep killing, and never be found. Missing persons would eventually turn up, but they would not say anything about being killed.

Maybe he was actually doing something good, by helping these refugees find a new home.

"Go sleep over it," the doctor said. "We can be good allies."

He gave Dunningan a smile, and then gently pushed Dunningan toward the tunnel that led back to the crypt.

Dunnigan smiled. ✷

Okello's Honeymoon

I proposed to Meg at the lakeside. We were sitting on a rock that jutted out onto the water, watching the sun drop behind a half-submerged canoe. The waves sang as they crashed onto the shore. Birds chirped as they hunted for fish. Mosquitoes and lake flies buzzed around us. It was just the two of us in the wilderness. I took out the ring and held it in front of her. It gleamed in the dying light of the day, like a true diamond, though it was a cheap aluminum piece of artwork that a friend had fashioned for me. She said yes.

It struck me as odd that I had proposed to a girl whose family I had never met. She said they lived in Merikit, a small town ten miles from my home, and that I would meet them during the kwanjula, the traditional marriage ceremony where I would pay her father a dowry. I brushed aside the alarm bells, and trusted everything she told me. I was madly in love.

We set a date. We would have two ceremonies. On a Friday, my family and I would go to her father's home and deliver the bridal gifts. The next day, we would go to church for a Christian wedding. But two weeks before the date, she changed her mind. She no longer wanted to marry me.

She had gone to visit her family to prepare the festivities. I did not expect to see her for several days, so when I heard her banging at my door in the dead of night, crying for me to open, I knew that something had gone terribly wrong. I dashed out of bed and snapped on the lights. Cockroaches fled into hiding. I ran stark naked to the front door, where a ghost confronted me.

I could not recognize her. I still cannot describe the color of her skin. She was the light skinned type, but that night she looked like an albino... No. Not albino. Her skin was transparent. I could see a net of blue veins crisscrossing under her skin. I never knew Africans could become this pale when frightened. Her face was a mess of tears and snot. Her lips bled where she had bitten them. Her scalp bled where she had yanked out the hair. Or maybe someone – *something* – had yanked out her hair. I tried to comfort her with a hug. She was cold and hard like a rock. She pushed me away and would not let me touch her again.

Not knowing how to handle the situation, I did not insist. I collapsed onto the sofa. She sat down beside me. Forgetting the moment, I nearly smiled in surprise. She had avoided sitting on that sofa for many months, after we discovered a rat family inside it. I killed the rats, but sofaphobia gripped her. She wanted a new set. I could not afford it. I was hoping my uncle would give us one as a wedding gift. That night she forgot about the rats and sat beside me. Something worse than a thousand rats had terrified her.

"Oh Boke, my love," was the only coherent thing she could say for about ten minutes. She did not use the tender name she gave me, Boo. She bit her fingers so hard they bled. I again tried to comfort her with a hug. She pushed me away and sat on the coffee table. Finally, she managed to utter a coherent sentence. "I cannot marry you."

I thought I had not heard right, but then, as if on cue, I heard a squeaking in the sofa and it struck me that another family of rats had found a home. All I could think of at that time was to buy poison to get rid of the pests.

She ran into the bedroom before I could say anything. I wanted to follow her. I could not move. Those four words had numbed me. *I cannot marry you.* She tottered out a short while later, dragging a hastily packed suitcase. A toothbrush, t-shirt, and make-up case dropped as she sped away. She did not bother to pick them up.

I lived on the first floor of a very old building. There were cracks on the wall, and the paint had peeled off. The window panes were made of wood. They were moldy and stank like rotten beans. I opened the window and looked down into Bazaar Street, which Indian traders had built in the 1930s. It now lay in a state of rot, silent and deserted, dark, the only illumination being the crescent moon that hung low in the horizon, just above the old houses like an evil eye grinning at me. Meg hurried down the road, an apparition vanishing into the moonlit darkness of the decaying town.

I tried to kill myself. I did not eat for three days. I drank several bottles of crude alcohol, a hot, 'kill-me-quick' stuff called lira lira. A small glass was enough to bomb me out of my senses. Sadly, rather than the grave, I woke up in the hospital, in the stinking, male ward with thirty other patients.

It's not our culture to send sick people flowers. We take sugar, fruits, food, or cash, things that can help, but I got a bouquet of roses from someone who signed her name as Nambi. Puzzled, I did not know what to do with the flowers, nor did the nurses, so we threw them away. Still, the name Nambi was forever burned into my brain.

Many friends visited me. They talked a lot of nonsense to comfort me. They said that at twenty five, I was too young to kill myself over a girl, that I would soon fall in love again and forget Meg. The only person I longed to see was Okello, my best friend since childhood. He worked at Coca Cola as a salesman and was away on a trip when Meg dropped the bomb. He would not have let me hit the bottle. When he came, he brought warmth into the ward. I smiled for the first time since being hospitalized. He did not smile back.

"Boke," he said. "Killing yourself over a girl is really stupid."

I stopped smiling. I did not like the tone of his voice. He was my friend. He was supposed to make me feel better. I wished I had used a quicker method like a rope.

"And getting angry over what I am going to tell you will be more stupid," he added. I frowned. His lips started to tremble. He cracked his knuckles as he struggled to stop his fingers from trembling. "It might, you know, be, you know, a bit unpleasant." The scar on his left cheek looked like a girlish dimple. It appeared to be grinning at me.

"What –"

"It's about Meg," he said quickly, cutting me short.

At the back of my mind I wished it were bad news, that a car crash had killed her. But I was also eager to hear that she wanted us to get back together. Okello waited a long time, driving me crazy with the suspense. I did not press him. I held my breath.

"I'm going to marry her."

I laughed. I thought it was a big joke meant to cheer me out of my depression.

"She, you know, came to me," he stuttered. Every muscle in his body now trembled. "She just, you know, came and said she, you know, loves me and wants to marry me. I don't know what happened to me. I don't know why I accepted. Maybe she, you know, gave me a love potion. Yes! That's it! She gave me a love potion and I fell madly in love with her."

I lunged at him. The IV tubes attached to my veins ripped off, blood and medicine splashed. I punched him. He fell to the floor. I fell on him. My fingers found his neck. I squeezed. He fought, but I had a firm grip. I squeezed, and squeezed. Other patients were screaming. Strong hands grabbed me, and wrench me off him. A nurse pricked me with a needle and everything went black.

#

After they discharged me, my younger brother came to watch over me for a few days. I tried to pull my life together, to get over Meg and Okello's betrayal and move on. I went back to work in a small cramped room at the back of a jute factory. The Indian bosses understood. They did not fire me for going absent without leave. A week's worth of work had accumulated. I buried myself in ledger books, and it helped take Meg off my mind. I smiled a lot. I told jokes a lot. At home, I watched movies or played scrabble with my brother. I did anything to stop myself from thinking about her. But one afternoon as we watched the X-Men, my cell phone rang. Reluctantly, I answered it.

"Hallo?" a woman said. "Hallo? May I know who I'm speaking to?"

"Who did you call?" I asked.

"I'm Nambi," she said. The name sent a jolt up my spine. Was this the stranger who had sent me flowers? "Are you Boke?" she added.

"What do you want?"

"To talk to you."

"About what?"

"Meg."

"Screw you." I switched off the phone.

After nearly ten minutes, my brother's phone rang. He answered it. I knew instinctively that it was Nambi. I wondered how she got our numbers. As he listened to her, a strange expression came over his face. He gave me the phone to me. I didn't take it.

"This is weird," he said. "Better listen to her."

Reluctantly, I took the phone.

"I'm at The Mayors," she said. "Please join me. There are things about Meg that I want to tell you."

The Mayors was a restaurant-cum-bar at the end of the street. I frequented it to watch European football games, and to drink with Okello and the boys. Though it was my favorite hang-out, I did not want to ever set my foot in it again. Meg and I first met in there. She had turned up from nowhere, one day, looking for a job, and the manager hired her as a waiter. She had lived in a small room at the back with three other girls until she moved in with me. She still worked at there, but had asked for leave to prepare for her wedding with Okello. Did Nambi know this? Why did she want us to meet there? Why did she not come to my home?

"I don't want to know anything about her," I said.

"She truly loves you," she said. "She dumped you after she discovered what would happen to her husband during the honeymoon. She didn't want you to suffer."

"I don't want to know," I said, though my mouth had gone dry.

"Do you know that her entire family is dead?"

"What?"

"Come to The Mayors. I'll tell you how they died."

"Her parents are alive," I said. "They live in Merikit."

"Did you actually meet them?" She gave me a few seconds to think about that before going on. "I'm her cousin. She lived with us after her family died. I am dead too, but I'm fed up of being dead. Meg wants to be a living dead too, but she doesn't know what she's getting herself into. Please come. Maybe we can stop her. Maybe we can save your friend.

"You see, she needs to be married in a church for it to work. She has to do it before the next rains, which is in two months. She picked Okello because–"

A strange sound interrupted her. Later, I discovered it was the sound of a fork stabbing her throat. I heard the gurgling, as blood spurt out of her severed neck. Her phone fell to the floor, ending the call.

I ran to The Mayors.

As I reached it, I heard screams. Two waitresses, Meg's workmates, fled out of the door, yelling at the top of their voices. I dashed in. It was not a large room, only big enough for six tables, with old and musty furniture infested with cockroaches. A torn plastic carpet was spread on the wooden floor. It being late afternoon, the place was almost empty. The lunch-time crowd had gone, and the evening revelers had not yet arrived. Three men stood uncertainly around a woman who lay on the floor. One of them, George, the manager, was shouting into the phone, maybe calling the police, maybe asking for a car to take the woman to hospital.

She was still alive. Her legs twitched. She lay on her back, weakly fighting a fork that was buried deep in her throat. She would be gone in a few more seconds. Her eyes stared blankly at the giant ceiling fan that rotated in slow motion. Blood bubbled on her neck and pooled around her, soaking the wooden floor. It looked like blackish goo. And it stank.

Shortly after I walked in, she gave up the struggle and went limp. Her fingers slid off the fork. The light went out of her eyes. A sudden silence fell upon the room. George stopped talking on the phone. I looked at the dead eyes and I knew that an evil force had killed her for trying to warn me about Meg.

#

The police came an hour later. They did not find any identification papers on the body. Her phone revealed no clues either, it had no numbers apart from the two she dialed. Mine, and my brother's. I told Sergeant Jamil, the officer in charge of the Criminal Investigations Department, everything she had told me. He did not believe a word of it.

"Did you kill her as some sort of revenge because Meg left you?" he asked.

I did not answer his senseless question. The other witnesses testified as to what exactly happened. The woman walked into the restaurant and asked for food. The food came. She did not touch it. She, instead, made a call. No one bothered her. They did not overhear what she said because she talked in a low voice, and she sat away from everyone else. Suddenly, according to George, who was ogling her, the fork jumped off the table and dove into her throat.

The detective did not believe him either. He tapped the fork with a pen. "How can we arrest a fork?" he said, giving George a contemptuous smile.

It did not help us that Meg worked here, though she was absent that day, preparing for her wedding. The sergeant interrogated her over the phone. She denied knowing the dead woman. She said I made up all these things to spoil her love with Okello. The policeman believed her. He threw us into jail. Me, George, the two waitresses, the two men I found at the restaurant, we all ended up behind bars.

"You will rot there unless you tell us the truth," Sergeant Jamil said.

Then, the next day, he suddenly dropped all charges against us. He was frightened. Apparently, the pathologist had noticed something strange in Nambi's body. Her flesh was not 'fresh', yet not rotten. It looked like stale beef with mold. It had traces of maggots. He thought that at one time her body had started to decompose, but then something stopped the decomposition. Her body became new, trapping the maggots in its rebirth. Upon making this discovery, the doctor fled from the hospital. He rushed to the nearest Church to pray for protection, convinced that Nambi was an evil creature.

Zombie, was all I could think of. But I had seen the movies. Nambi was a pretty woman, an intelligent being who walked into a restaurant and ordered fish stewed in groundnut sauce. How could she be a zombie? Did it have anything to do with the strange stories of cannibalism in the central and western parts of the country, where abasezi resurrect dead bodies to work as slaves, and to be eaten?

#

I tried digging into Meg's past. I went to Merikit town and asked around. Her father's name, she had said, was Oundo Omiel. No one knew him. Merikit was a small rural trading centre where everyone knew everyone. If her family really lived there, someone would have known her father.

I was baffled, a few days later, when I met with Okello's younger brother. He told me that Meg was taking Okello and some of his family to Merikit for the kwanjula ceremony. They would pay a dowry of ten heads of cattle. Meg's family had insisted that the groom bring no more than ten people. Strict demands were common in kwanjula. However, limiting visitors to ten was out of the ordinary, especially since the two families lived within the same district.

On the wedding day, I hired a motorcycle and discreetly followed Okello's entourage of two saloon cars and a lorry carrying ten heads of cattle. Just before reaching Merikit town, they turned off the road into a narrow footpath. I followed them through a small eucalyptus forest, and then to a homestead hidden inside a maze garden. I abandoned the motorcycle in the forest and tiptoed through the garden to the compound. I hid behind a shrub and examined the homestead. It had a red brick house with a green roof, and three mud huts painted red, black and white with clay and ash. Two tents had been set up for the ceremony. The groom's family sat in one, the women in gomesis and the men in kanzus and coats. About fifty people sat in the other. Was this Meg's family?

I had achieved my objective. I now knew where her family lived.

I raced back to Merikit town. The bars were full that Saturday afternoon. People sat on the pavements in small circles around pots, sucking malwa beer from long tubes. About thirty youths danced in the street, beside a giant music speaker that boomed Brenda Fassie's Wedding Day. An old mechanic sat alone under a tree, mending a bicycle, oblivious to the festivities in the town. I had talked to him in my previous visit. I now walked up to him, and asked him about the homestead behind the eucalyptus forest.

"Is that the man you were asking about?" he said.

I nodded.

"And you went to his home?"

I again nodded. "My friend is there right now, in a kwanjula."

The man's eyes grew several inches larger. His mouth dropped open. His skin seemed to grow several shades darker.

"No," he said. It came out as a sigh. "Nobody lives there."

"No," I said. "Maybe we are talking about different homesteads. I saw people there. They are having a kwanjula party."

"That family died a long time ago," the mechanic whispered. "The father, mother, the children, soldiers killed them all during Obote's regime. Only one girl survived. Margret. That was her name. No one knows where she is. That homestead has been in ruins ever since. If you saw people there, then you have seen ghosts."

"I think we are talking about different homesteads," I said, and walked away from the man. I asked three other people, and they told me the same thing. I became confused.

I went back to Meg's home. Before I could reach the eucalyptus forest, I heard vehicles. I hid in the bush. Okello's entourage passed by. I frowned. It had been barely two hours since they arrived. The ceremony could not be over. It normally lasted at least six hours. After they had gone, I waited until I could not hear the vehicles again, and then proceeded into the forest.

The moment I walked out of the other side of the forest, I began to believe what the old mechanic had told me. Where I had seen a maze garden, nothing grew but a withered bush. For a moment I thought I had taken a wrong turn in the forest. I retraced my footsteps, but there was only one path from the main road through the eucalyptus trees. The maze garden had vanished. In its place was shriveled, yellow grass.

I could see the homestead in the distance. It was in ruins. Unable to believe, thinking my eyes were playing tricks on me, I went closer. My mouth tasted as though it was filled with salt. My knees were weak. I could not feel my feet. The footpath petered out about ten meters from the homestead. I waded through a thick, waist-high bush. The compound was empty, and overgrown with yellowed grass. The brick house had crumbled. The roof had fallen away. A small tree had grown, and died, inside one of the rooms. Its bare branches hung above the broken walls. The three mud huts now looked like anthills. There was not a living thing in sight. The vegetation looked as though a severe drought had scorched the land. No insects flew about. No birds sang. No lizards. No frogs. Not even a breeze blew.

#

I tried to warn to Okello. I called him and explained that I had something very important to say. He agreed to meet at my home. He said our friendship was too deep to be broken by a mere woman, who might leave him after a few years. When I told him what I had found in Merikit, even after I showed him the photos I had taken with my phone's camera, his face darkened. His lips became tight.

"Boke," he said. "I know how you feel. I understand if you never forgive me. But I'll give you one piece of advice. Forget us. Move on with your life."

With that, he drained his beer, belched, muttered a thank you and walked out. I was left staring sheepishly at my bottle.

#

They had a Christian wedding a week after the kwanjula. I did not go. That same evening as the two families and many friends partied, at about eight o'clock, Meg and Okello vanished. I heard about it the next day from our mutual friends. 'You were right,' they told me. 'Something terrible has happened to Okello.' The two families however did not think much of it. They refused to involve the police. Then, six days later, Okello's younger brother came to see me.

"We should have listened to you," he said. "I fear Okello is dead."

It happened during the 'dress change' ritual, when both the bride and groom discard the costumes they wore in church and change into party clothes. Meg and Okello left their guests in the gardens of Rock Hotel, the best in town, and went into the honeymoon suite. They never came out. After an hour of knocking on the door, Okello's brother forced it open. He found a note on the bed, in Okello's handwriting. It simply said, 'Don't worry. We are on honeymoon.' They had not yet cut the cake. The speeches had not been made. The gifts were undelivered. Both their phones were off, and for the next several days no one was able to contact them.

"Maybe they'll turn up okay," I said, trying to sound hopeful, but I knew something terrible had happened. *She dumped you after she learnt what would happen to her husband*, Nambi had said.

"Let's go to her home," Okello's brother said. He was hardly twenty years, still a student, with a small goatee beard. His name was Opus.

I shook my head. "There is nobody there," I said. I showed him the photos of the ruins. He looked at the photos for a long time, and quietly handed me back the phone.

"I don't know where you took that picture," he said, "but it wasn't at her home."

"You still don't believe me," I said.

"I do," Opus said. "My brother is missing. I believe you."

"Maybe the police will help," I said.

"They say there is no evidence of a crime, so they cannot get involved. My parents are upset but they are not taking any action. They think there is no cause to worry. But I know there is a big problem. I can feel it. You know it too. Please, help me. We have to find him."

The only clue we had was the homestead.

Six days was a long time. Anything could have happened in that time. But then, there was a small chance that we could still save him. I hired a motorcycle and we raced off to Merikit. We arrived at about five pm. Just as I found it earlier, the homestead was in ruins.

"This is witchcraft," Opus said. "We had a party here just last week."

"I told you so," I said.

His pants darkened. He had pissed on himself. He fled from the homestead, ran very fast back up the path into the eucalyptus forest, not looking back. I wanted to run too, but if I did I would never find out what happened to Okello. We had been friends since childhood. I still loved him. If he were dead, or hurt in anyway, I had to bring Meg to justice.

I began to search. I did not know what to look for. I went through the brick house. Empty. Nothing but shriveled weeds. The mud huts were empty too. I searched the withered bushes, and was about to give up when I saw another footpath. It was overgrown. I followed it with difficulty. It led to a huge rock, twenty feet high, sculpted to look like an onion. I knew at once that it held the key to the mystery. The country was littered with beautiful rocks, artworks of nature that could be mistaken for man-made artifacts. Some still bore relics from Stone Age people, paintings, musical instruments, tools. This onion-shaped structure, with a surface as smooth as marble, could not be a natural phenomenon. The setting sun fell upon it, painting it a strange yellow. A thin strip of red light, about four feet long and running vertically, flickered on its surface. It was so straight that I thought of lamplight shining through a crack on a door.

I tapped the rock and received an echo. It was hollow. I tapped again, and the rock began to move. I jumped back, preparing to flee, when it struck me that the rock was not moving. Rather, a portion of it was opening, like a sliding door with a rattling sound, revealing a candlelit cave. A man stood at the entrance, still in his wedding suit. Okello. A strong, sweet perfume came from the room behind him.

His clothes were dirty and stained with blood, his hair matted and knotted. His eyes were bloodshot, bulging out of their sockets like those of an alien. His lips had cracked and were bleeding.

"Did you come to finish me off?" he croaked, his voice sounding like dry leaves.

I did not understand him. He ducked back into the rock and the door started to close, moving so slowly. I looked into the cave. Hundreds of candles lined the walls, lighting it up. I saw a white bundle on the floor. Was that Meg in her bridal gown? Was she asleep, or dead? Before I knew what I was doing, I dashed into the cave, squeezing myself through the tiny space as the door closed.

Okello cursed.

The cave had a diameter of about twenty feet. The smoke from the candles hung low like thin mist. The sweet smell was overpowering. A clock chimed on the wall, tick-tock-tick-tock, booming like a beating heart. In the middle of the floor, Meg lay supine on a mat in her wedding gown, the veil thrown over her face. She was so still and stiff. One look at her face and I knew she was dead. Several days dead. I jumped away in terror.

"She's not dead," he said. "She's only sleeping."

What madness, I thought. Can he not see the maggots crawling in her eyes?

I ran for the door, which was nothing but a slab of rock. No handle. No hinges. I could not open it. I tried to push it open. I tried to pull it. It would not budge.

"Open this door!" I screamed at Okello.

He was lost in his own misery. He sat down, beating his head with his fists, muttering curses as he cried.

"Why did you come in," he said. "You've ruined everything. She was going to resurrect. Tonight at midnight. She was going to come back to life. But you've ruined it. I was supposed to wait alone. No one else was supposed to enter the shrine. But you've fucked it up."

I looked at Okello, and for the first time I wondered how she had convinced him to take part in her evil scheme. What love potion was so powerful it could turn an intelligent fellow into a puppet? *She dumped you because she loves you.* She did not want me to suffer in her quest to become a living dead. Was this what Nambi meant, or did something worse await Okello?

"When I heard the knocks I thought it was the old man and I thought it was okay to open but it was you. Fuck you, Boke. Did you come to kill me?"

"No," I said. "I came with Opus to save you."

"Liar," he said. "You bewitched me. You wanted to kill me but she saved my life. She paid for my life with her own life and she would be dead for only six days and then come back to life but you've ruined it."

Dead for six days? That meant she had died on their wedding night.

"Please Okello," I said. "Open the door. Let me go."

He gave me a sad smile. "No," he said. "You stay. When the old man comes I'll tell him that you forced your way in then maybe I can get a second chance to bring her back to life."

#

We waited for the old man. As time passed, Okello told me his honeymoon tale. I sat on the warm floor, dumbfounded, listening in a hypnotic state.

On the wedding night, when they went into the room to change, he suddenly felt a sharp pain in his stomach, fire erupted somewhere inside and consumed him. He fell to the floor, screaming in agony. His bride held him in her arms, comforting him, shouting for the doctor, telling him it would be alright. He passed out.

"What about the note you wrote," I interrupted him.

"What note?" he said.

"You left a note on the bed. It said 'don't worry. We are on our honeymoon.'"

"I left no note," he said. "I fell sick and passed out."

He woke up in the cave, on the papyrus mat, to the blinding glare of candles and a suffocating sweet smell. The pain had gone. Meg sat next to him, her arms wrapped around her knees, tears on her face.

"What happened?" he asked her. "Where am I?"

"In a witchdoctor's shrine," she replied. "We took you to hospital but the doctors couldn't help. So we rushed you here. You nearly died. You had a big wound in your stomach." Okello checked his tummy, and sure enough it had a large wound, as though he had been operated upon. "Boke did witchcraft on you. He was jealous of you. He wanted to kill you. But jajja saved your life."

Meg broke down and wept. Okello hugged her.

"I have to pay for your cure with my life," she added.

"What do you mean?" he said.

"It's only for a few days. He assured me I'll be dead only for a few days and after six days I'll resurrect. Please be strong. It's the only way."

"Meg, what are you talking about?"

She yelped in pain. A severe headache attacked her. It had peculiar characteristics. It affected only one side of her head at a time. First, it was the right side. Then the pain shifted to the left side. For an hour, the pain seesawed in her head until it finally exploded. A fire burned her brain. Her nose bled and stained the white gown. At ten to midnight, she asked for the time. He replied after a glance at the clock.

"I'm going to die," she cried. She grabbed his hands. Her nails sank into his flesh. "I'm going to die at midnight."

The clock started to tick. He was sure it was not ticking before. It was so loud it echoed all over the cave, each tick banging into his skull like a hammer.

"Oh Meg," he said, wiping sweat, blood and tears off her face. "I'll find another doctor."

But the clock struck midnight. Meg died.

Okello held her in his arms, too shocked to do anything. Too shocked to cry. He did not realize the old man had entered the room until he heard him clear his throat. Okello looked up, and saw a face as black as soot, a bald head with a thick, white beard. He wore nothing but bark cloth. Dozens of necklaces made out of bones and shells hung around his neck. His arms and ankles were decorated with bracelets made of animal skins.

"She'll be alright," the old man said.

“She’s dead,” Okello cried.

“It’s the jajjas,” the old man said. “They saved your life so they asked for hers in return, but only for a short while. She’ll resurrect on Friday at midnight if you do exactly as I say.”

Okello believed the old witch. He believed his wife would resurrect. He followed the instructions meticulously. He kept vigil by her deathbed. Every midnight, he smeared her body with a special oil, which the ancient Egyptians used to mummify their dead. Every hour he knelt beside the corpse and told her how much he loved her. No one else could be in the shrine with him. He could only leave it only at nine o’clock in the morning, to use the bathroom or to get food, which the old man left outside. He ate nothing but cow milk and blood. The smoke swirled around him. The sweet smell encouraged him. Rigor stiffness held the corpse. A net of ghastly blue veins appeared on her skin, which was now yellowish and transparent. He could see the rot in her flesh, the maggots crawling under the skin. Her eyes bulged out of their sockets and looked like two eggs on her face. The pupils disappeared, leaving a dead white terror glaring, with maggots swimming in it like fish in a glass bowl. Okello braved the horrors and patiently waited for this hideous creature to come back alive. He had a lot of hope until I walked into the shrine.

#

Okello did not know how to contact the old man. He could only wait for him to show up. If he did not come at midnight, when Meg was supposed to resurrect, he would come the following day at nine to bring him food. At a loss of what else to do, Okello continued with the rituals. He knelt by her side every hour and said how much he loved her.

The minutes ticked away. Okello sat by the corpse, restive. I kept a good distance away by the door, which was of no use for I could not get out. Only a magic word could open it. Okello knew the password. He would not tell it to me. The noisy clock filled the night with a creepy tick tock tick that stressed the silence. The candlelight made the shadows dance. The smoke made the room spooky. We sat still. We waited.

At nine, just after the clock's ninth dong, and just after he told the dead thing how much he loved it, Okello yelled and darted away from the corpse.

"Meg – she spoke – Meg spoke! Did you – did you hear?" I had not heard anything but the clock. "She said she loves me too. She spoke." He laughed. It sounded like the insane clash of metals. "Maybe it will still work," he said. "Maybe she'll still come back to life."

At ten, he let out another shrill scream. "Look! Look!" He bounced like a ball as he pointed at the corpse. "She moved." I had not seen anything. "Look! Again!" I turned to the corpse. It was stiff on the mat. "She's waving." But the corpse was not moving at all. "She's coming back," he said into my face. "Two hours left."

Eleven o'clock. Okello grabbed me by the arms and dragged me to the corpse. For one who looked sick and starving, he had enough strength to force me to look at the dead body. It had changed. Its eyes were back to normal size. The yellow complexion and the blue veins had disappeared from her skin. I could no longer see the rot and the maggots in her flesh. It now looked like Meg. "See? See? One hour left."

One very long hour.

We waited. Okello paced about, gesticulating, whispering to himself, panting. I still sat by the door, trying to stay calm, sweating profusely. We waited. Midnight drew closer, closer. Okello's pacing became frantic, his gesticulations violent. The ticking got louder. I put my fingers in my ears to shut out the noise but it only got louder, louder – *louder*! Until finally the clock started to dong – once, twice, thrice. We froze, our eyes glued to the corpse – six times, seven times, eight times – each dong echoed in the cave with an icy terror – twelve dongs – midnight.

Meg woke up. Like one startled out of sleep by a nightmare, she stood up, confused, frightened. Alive.

"Meg," Okello whispered. I was flat against the wall, trembling. "Meg." Okello inched towards her, mesmerized, arms outstretched to hug her. "Meg."

Just when he thought everything would be alright after all, something started to happen to her. Her pupils vanished, and the dead white terror returned. Fangs sprang out of her mouth, claws shot out of her fingers and toes, hair sprout out of her face. Even before she completed the transition into a beast, she attacked. With a demonic cat's shriek, she lunged at Okello. They tumbled onto the floor, wrestling. She had a firm grip on his neck and she did not stop squeezing, her claws digging into his flesh, drawing blood. And as Okello's life seeped out, she continued to transform into a cat-like creature.

I snatched a candle and torched her gown. She burst into flames. She rolled off Okello to fight the fire. She tried to rip off the burning gown, but the oil he had smeared on her body was highly flammable and it had soaked in. Her hair caught fire too. She fell to the floor, a burning mess, screaming, twitching.

Struggling to breathe, blood pouring out of his neck, Okello barely managed to utter the magic word. The door slid open. We staggered out, and fled from the cave. We ran until we reached the ruined homestead, where I had left the motorcycle. We sped back to town.

#

Okello survived. There are scars on his neck and stomach, souvenirs from his first marriage. He has never stopped thanking me for saving his life.

When the residents of Merikit heard our tale, they mobilized and under the leadership of a shaman and set the homestead alight, burning everything. Meg's body was in the cave, charred. Nobody touched it. Instead, they rigged dynamite around the onion-shaped rock and blew it up.

No one caught sight of any of the living dead. The photographs that were taken during the wedding were of no use. They faded away leaving nothing but white blankness on the paper. They probably slipped away to another area, or maybe they are still in the vicinity. Maybe some people in the mob who torched up the homestead were living dead too. We shall never know. ✷

A Bloodline of Blades

Mozze's tribe lived in caves in a mountain on the fringe of the empire. They were tall and had the color of burnt wood. They wore long dreadlocks decorated with brightly colored beads. The peak of their mountain looked like a white cloud in the blue sky. Under the full moon, it turned into a gleaming pearl that inspired them to make merry all night long.

Mozze looked forward to the next full moon, which coincided with the Elephant Festival. He dreamt of winning the Green Drum with his new song, mpenzi moja, a love ballad about a poor belle and a prince. He had practiced it for many moons, tried it out on many instruments, until it flowed out of his soul like a bewitching stream sparkling in the moonlight. As the fiesta drew closer, he became restless, desperate, like a hanging man struggling to free the rope around his neck.

On a cold afternoon twelve days to the fete, as he roasted a giant rat in the kitchen of his cave, he hummed the new song. He had a sweet voice. It gave credit to the gossip that his real father was a musician. They said that his mother was already pregnant when she ran away from her husband, who her family had forced her to marry, to live with her forbidden lover. Mozze did not let the gossip distract him. His voice drifted with the smoke up the chimney, into the gardens above, where his wife, Mishash, milked a mbisi. He sang in rhythm to the sound of milk jetting into a clay bowl. But then, the music of her work stopped. She was listening to his song. He knew her eyes were closed in a swoon, and love was flowing through her veins like a fresh stream coming down the mountains after a long dry spell. He closed his eyes too, and let the lyrics waft up to her like the enchanted smoke of a djinni.

But their only child, Jez, suddenly broke the magic of the moment.

"Pa!" Jez screamed, his voice boomed down the chimney into the kitchen, drowning out Mozze's song. He was returning from the forest where he had gone to collect ritti leaves to feed the mbisi, and he had caught his mother swooning. "You are not a silly girl!"

Mozze went quiet. The contempt in the boy's voice made him regret the decision to go public with his music. But at that time, it had sounded like a good idea. His wife had just been barred from attending a cousin's wedding party. His was an isolated family, a pariah family, because he was an assassin. Mishash hated it. She urged him to do something about it. Music was the only solution he could think of. He believed it would show off his romantic side, give him a new image other than that of a blood thirsty monster. However, the moment he signed up for the contest, the gossip about his true father started, and it had poisoned his son.

"I belong to a family of real men!" Jez now shouted. "The sword is my destiny, not a useless drum!"

Mozze heard him smashing the ritti leaves onto the ground, and then stomping away.

He had to make his son understand the importance of his musical ambition. In another twelve moons, Jez would be old enough to marry, and he would have trouble finding a bride. No man would let his daughter marry into a family of assassins. The only way was for a girl to fall so madly in love that she defies her father, elopes, and gets disowned. That was how Mozze had found his wife. That was how their forefathers started families. In isolation. With curses from the girl's family. Mozze did not want it to happen to Jez. He wanted his family to be accepted, to join others in roaming from cave to cave, singing, dancing, telling stories, laughing and drinking yellow wine every Tukasday. Getting the chief to award him a green drum would be the first step in that direction. He had to make Jez understand.

He removed the rat from the fire, and walked out of the kitchen into a vast room draped in a myriad of crisscrossing lights. Gems and mirrors reflected a sunbeam that sneaked in through a crack on the mountainside, lighting up the cave with a dozen colors. A circular carpet lay in the middle of the room, inside a ring of three-legged stools. Here the family ate their meals, hosted the few visitors who came by, and made merry. Six caverns dug in the wall served as bedchambers, a bathing room, a granary and the kitchen. The cave was covered with paintings of animals, both real and imagined. The mountain elephant, the tribe's totem, dominated.

The entrance was only four feet high. Mozze had to crouch to get out into the warm, evening sunshine. He found Jez throwing knives at a tree. Jez did not acknowledge his father's presence. The sound of steel striking wood illustrated his fury.

Before Mozze could say a word, a rustling in the footpath below distracted him. He turned to see Hinko, the old innkeeper who lived at the foot of the mountain, struggling up the steep slope using a bamboo crutch, panting and sweating. Mozze wondered what was so important that the old man had to climb rather than send a messenger dove.

"Hinko," Mozze said. "What's the bad news?"

The old man forced out a smile in spite of the exhaustion.

"Ah," he said. "Can't a friend visit his neighbor these days?" He glanced at the tree to admire Jez's practice. The boy had thrown over a dozen knives into the bull's eye. "We sure have a new knife master."

"Tell Pa!" Jez said, as though his father was not present. "Instead of teaching me, he sings like a silly girl!"

Without giving them a chance to respond, Jez stomped away down the path like a sulking mbisi. Mozze sighed, and then he helped Hinko up the last steps into the cave. He returned to the kitchen, and resumed roasting the rat. Hinko took off his sheepskin coat and draped it on a hook, and then he sat on a stool near the door.

"Wine?" Mozze handed him a jug of the yellow drink made from bananas.

"No," Hinko said. "It indeed is bad news. I got visitors. Three Messengers."

Mozze's heart fell. He did not want any job before the full moon. He had waited for so long, practiced for so long. If he failed to perform during the Elephant Festival, when the entire nation gathered for a feast at the foot of the mountain, he would have to wait twelve moons for another chance to win the Green Drum.

"Who is it?"

"King Amara."

The name drove into Mozze's ears like a sword. He dropped the rat into the fire, splashing embers. Hinko shot out of his stool to save it. He dug it out of the fire, scalding his fingers, and dumped it onto a large, wooden tray.

"King Amara?" Mozze whispered. His throat was dry, his voice hoarse.

"The pay is very high," Hinko said, licking his fingers to ease the pain. "A thousand gold bars. Two-fifty now, the rest after the job. It must be done before the Elephant Festival."

Why?

Mozze rose to his feet. His knees felt weak. He took a sword off a hook on the wall, and stared at his image in the blade like a devotee staring at a holy statue. Whenever he saw his reflection, he saw his father, the swordsman, who taught him how to use a knife before showing him how to handle a spoon. The swordsman who killed Kwekwe the evil wizard, thereby bringing peace to all kingdoms. And who, rumor said, was not his real father. He often found consolation and reassurance in the memories the mirror evoked. But now, looking into the blade, he could not remember what his father had looked like. Mozze dropped the sword as though it had turned into a snake.

"No," he whispered.

"You've killed kings before," Hinko said. "Three kings. You killed Rampo whose guards were two-headed wolves. Who else has killed half a dozen two-headed wolves in a single fight?"

Rabbit ears! It struck Mozze so suddenly that lisis set his legs on fire. He slumped to the floor in agony, fumbled for the green, wooden vial in his undergarments and took a sip off it. In an instant, the pain vanished, but it left him exhausted. He sat up, panting.

"Is it lisis? Has it eaten your legs so much that you can't work anymore?"

Mozze shook his head. "Why must it be done before the festival?"

It took Hinko a few heartbeats to comprehend the conspiracy. "Prince Manet!"

Mozze nodded. King Amara ruled over all the seventy tribes, though each tribe was autonomous and sub-ruled by a chief. The king had two sons. The young one was Palla, the favorite.

He would be crowned heir during the Elephant Festival. The eldest was Manet, but he could not rule for he had married a rabbit-eared woman. However, if the king died heirless, the chiefs would have no choice but crown his eldest son, Manet, as the law required.

"Ow no," Hinko said. "That rabbit-eared creature will become our queen!"

"Obscene."

"But will the chiefs accept a rabbit-eared queen?"

"Probably. Many fools today think those creatures are like us."

"Ow no. How can we bow down to rabbit-ears?"

"We must warn the king."

"No, Pa," Jez said.

Startled, Mozze and Hinko turned to see the boy at the kitchen entry, flipping a knife. The lights from the living room illuminated the green beads on his dreadlocks, conjuring the picture of a strange crown.

"You must take this offer."

Mozze's eyes flushed red in anger. "When did you start telling me what to do?"

"I'm no longer a boy," Jez took out a second dagger and started to juggle. "I'm old enough to marry."

"The stupidity of youth," Hinko said.

"Why won't you do it?" Jez said.

"In this cave," Mozze said, "we kill only the evil. King Amara is not evil."

"Really?" Jez said. "Why then did he let his son marry a rabbit-eared creature?"

Mozze opened his mouth to retort, but he realized the boy had trapped him in his own argument. He saw Jez wipe his mouth to hide a smile of triumph.

"This is not about good kings and bad kings," Jez said. "It's about a man running away from his duty because he wants to sing."

"Shut up!" Mozze said.

"If you like singing so much, why didn't you grow up in that musician's cave?"

"Ow no," Hinko said.

"Jez!" Mishash's voice screeched down the chimney. "Shut up or I'll spank you!"

"You shut up!" Jez shouted back at her. "I'm a man now!"

"Ow no," Hinko said, his mouth hanging open.

The fire lit up Mozze's face, making it seem blacker than normal. His eyes glowed with anger.

"I'll soon inherit this cave," Jez said. "I must protect its reputation."

Mozze did not know how to respond. A few heartbeats of silence passed, the crackling of the fire accentuated the tension in the room. Finally, without another word, Jez walked away.

#

For the first time in his life, Jez did not sleep in the cave. His parents worried about him all night. Mishash fell asleep on Mozze's chest, her face wet with tears. Shortly after sunrise, as Mozze prepared a breakfast of millet bread and mbisi milk, a dove flew down the chimney and vomited a message from Hinko.

"I found the messengers gone," the note said. "Jez offered them his services."

A sudden surge of lisis seared Mozze's legs, as though he had stepped on live coals. He crumbled to the floor with a yelp. He rushed for the vial in his undergarments, and took a sip for an instant remedy. The pain died. The exhaustion fell in. The dove watched with bored eyes, waiting for him to chant the spells to send a reply.

"I had to warn the king," the note continued. "Sorry. It'll be impossible for Jez."

The messenger doves had a disadvantage. It was easy to steal the notes they carried. All the conspirators had to do was hire a wizard to read the doves heading into the palace and they would have intercepted the warning. But they did not, which indicated that they were careless and amateurish. Now that the king knew, Hinko would get a hundred gold bars as a reward for his loyalty, but Jez would certainly die.

Mishash walked into the kitchen. She looked very old, the beads in her dreadlocks shone in the myriad of colored lights that gave the room a somber atmosphere. She sat beside him. He wrapped his arms around her, offering comfort in the warmth of his body, wishing he could sing to assure her that everything was all right.

"What happened to Jez?"

"He thinks he can kill the king."

Her tears fell onto his shoulder like warm raindrops. "Please, save him."

#

Mozze set out at noon. He borrowed a horse from Hinko's inn and rode fast to the city, reaching it just after sundown. The city lights looked like a million candles glowing on a dark lake around a little mountain. The palace stood on top of the little mountain, sparkling like a crown of stars, creating the illusion of a brilliant rainbow.

He shared a cheap hotel room with twelve other men. As he

ate supper, he eavesdropped on their conversations. They spoke of the sudden increase in palace security. Guards doubled. Visitors screened more carefully, less than half the usual number allowed in. A lot of theories floated about, but when someone blamed the rabbit-eared folk, the room fell silent.

"Why did Amara invite them into our kingdom?" the speaker said. "Because his son fell in love? Now they want to kill him. We must drive them back into the forest."

All night, Mozze puzzled over how to find his son. A search from inn to inn would be futile. He would need thirty days for that, yet the festival was eleven days away. That meant ten nights for Jez to attempt the assassination. It had to be night because Jez, being young and inexperienced, would want to sneak in like a thief. He would choose a time just before the first cock crow, when the world is asleep and the guards exhausted. Jez would think daytime, which a skilled assassin would prefer, is too risky.

Mozze went to the palace the next day. A long, closely guarded drawbridge provided the only access. A moat as deep and wide as a river flowed around the wall. Boatloads of soldiers patrolled the moat, while hundreds more kept watch on the wall. He suffered the scrutiny of three sets of guards. They searched him thoroughly until they were satisfied that he was merely visiting the temple of Nyamwiru, the goddess of fertility. When he finally passed through the golden gate, he felt exhausted and naked.

The palace had two sections. Commoners were restricted to the outer segment, where the guards and staff lived, and where Nyamwiru's temple stood. A second wall enclosed the royal level. Mozze spent the day in the outer part, trying to figure out how his son would break into the royal section.

He decided it had to be through the garden, which had enough trees, flowers, fountains and statues to provide many hiding places. The rest of the commoner's section was too open and well lit, or full of the families of two thousand guards and palace employees. Moreover, at night couples sneaked into the garden to make love in the aphrodisiac aroma of the flowers, an open secret that Jez would seek to exploit.

This little forest had to be it. The problem would be to get past the hundreds of guards patrolling the moat and the outer wall.

A naïve person might get in during the day and hide in the garden until night. The guards however kept meticulous records. They would know if someone went in and never came out. They would search the garden until they found the intruder.

The second night in the city, Mozze crept up a tree to study the behavior of the guards who patrolled the wall. The bright lights made it easy to watch the wall and the moat, but impossible for anyone to sneak past the guards.

After a while, he searched the bushes and the trees, certain that Jez was somewhere nearby, looking for a way to beat the guards. He searched until dawn but he failed to find his son. For the next several days, he scoured inns near the palace, and every night he returned to the garden wall and searched with ever increasing despair. In vain. Then it happened, two nights before the festival.

A shadow walked to the moat, waving a handkerchief. Mozze recognized his son from the sparkle of green beads on his dreadlocks. He slipped down the tree and hurried after him, sword drawn, convinced that Jez planned to fight his way into the palace. A foolish act, for no single man could fight his way past a hundred guards on a wall.

"Jez!" he whispered as he ran. "Stop!" His voice was lost in the darkness.

A canoe approached Jez. Mozze could not run fast enough for he was trying to keep himself hidden and silent. He knew Jez could kill all six men on the boat with his knives before they got to him, but a barrage of arrows from the wall would bury him. Then, a strange thing happened. The canoe stopped. Jez climbed in.

Confused, Mozze crouched behind a shrub and watched the boat take his son to the other side. Questions ran through his mind. How did he connive with the palace guards? Are these Prince Manet's men? How could he save the king without putting his son's life in danger?

The guards on the wall threw down a rope ladder. Jez climbed up.

Mozze could not let him vanish, for then it would mean the loss of all hope. The king would die and then - and then the conspirators would turn against Jez! The best way is for an assassin to work alone, to find his own way in and out. By accepting this kind of help, Jez had placed himself totally under the mercy of the evil prince, and yet, if it became known that Manet hired an assassin to kill his father, Manet would lose the crown. Manet could not let that happen. He would have to kill Jez to destroy all evidence against him.

Jez went over the wall.

Mozze jumped into the moat and swam fast underwater. When he came up for air, a guard saw him. He vanished before the guard could shoot, but the next time he surfaced, arrows plopped into the water all around him. He vanished and resurfaced at the other bank, waving a hanky desperately. The shooting stopped.

Soldiers jumped off the canoe and drew their swords. Mozze

spread out both arms in surrender. They disarmed him.

"I'm with him," he said. "Didn't he tell you?"

The guards looked at each other in confusion. They talked in gestures with the men on the wall, who then threw down the rope ladder.

Mozze climbed. His old body could not go as fast as Jez had. At the top, he faced a dozen swords. One belonged to a highly ranked jessi, the green feather on his armor identified him as a maimai commander with a hundred warriors in his fighting unit.

"Who are you?" the maimai said.

"I'm with him," Mozze said.

"You can't be with him. It's his bobotong night with Sarrie."

Bobotong? Mozze smiled to hide the shock.

Seven nights to a marriage, the bride and groom perform the bobotong ritual to test the compatibility of their fates. Under arranged marriages, where parents decide who their children should marry, astrologers match the two fates and then the couples do the ritual in the presence of an aunt to confirm the astrologer's divination. But in naya marriages, where love unites the two, they do it in secret to assure themselves that their fates are compatible before visiting the astrologer, and then announcing their marriage.

How did Jez convince them that he only wanted to see a girl? Or is that the cover story in case someone caught them helping the assassin?

"You have ten heartbeats to live," the commander said.

"I'm his father."

"Huh?"

"Yes, I am. Look at my face."

The maimai studied Mozze's face under the torchlight. Mozze

held his breath until he saw the maimai's face relaxing. He had seen the resemblance.

"Why are you following him?"

Mozze's smile widened as the swords pressed into his neck. He smiled to hide his terror. He took a backward step, but the swords maintained pressure on his skin. Another step and he would fall to death.

"I want him to marry," he fumbled for an answer. "If he fails to please her, she'll think he isn't meant for her. And he'll fail because – because he's cursed. He needs a charm. He forgot it. I followed him to give it to him." He fished out the wooden vial of lisis medicine and gave it to the jessi. "Here. Take it to him. I'll go back down."

The commander did not take the vial.

"The flowers can help him," he said.

"No. The flowers work for normal men. He is cursed. Please, take it to him."

Mozze placed the bottle at the jessi's feet and started to go back down the rope.

"Wait," the maimai said. "Sarrie's father is my friend. You see there's this scare in the palace – but who am I to deny lovers their happiness? I checked your son. He's only a harmless, love sick boy."

Mozze thought of the thirty-six finger length knives in his son's vest, cleverly hidden under the sheep wool shirt. If the guards had asked Jez to remove his shirt, they would have seen his weapons.

"We can't leave our stations," the maimai said. "You take it to him. They are over there." He pointed at the giant statue of a two-headed wolf whose eyes shone red in the darkness.

Mozze did not know how fast his heart was beating until he climbed down into the flower garden. His hands trembled. He had never used deceit before. He always relied on his sword. He wanted to chide Jez, Who is the silly little girl? Who tells lies rather than use a sword like a real man? Yet he felt angry with himself for failing to make a proper assassin out of his son.

Thick darkness lay under the wolf's statue. Mozze could not see Jez. He searched hard, whispering urgently, and was just about to give up when he found a girl hidden under a paw. She was bound and gagged, drugged into a deep sleep.

Had Jez used a love potion to make her fall so madly in love with him in so short a time? Nothing else made sense. But how far would the bobotong lie take Jez? Certainly not into the king's chambers.

Beside the girl was a bundle of clothing, which Mozze recognized as his son's. Jez then had gone into the royal level in disguise. What disguise? A jessi? A palace worker? Mozze suddenly realized the futility of his efforts. He crumbled to the ground, defeated. Jez had vanished. Maybe he would succeed in killing the king and allow a rabbit-eared creature to become queen. Maybe he would fail, get captured and hanged. Whatever happens, Jez's rebellion had exposed Mozze's failure, both as a father and a mentor to his son. Never in their bloodline had a son rebelled to inherit the cave. The thought provoked such a severe lisis attack that he yelped out in pain.

"What's that?" a voice said.

"Sarrie and her lover," another replied.

"That's not the sound of lovemaking."

"It is."

"It isn't!"

Mozze took a long sip from the vial. He forced himself to shut up, to sit so still and not make any noise.

"Hear that?"

"It stopped."

"Isn't that strange?"

The pain ceased but exhaustion gripped Mozze as if he had just run up a steep slope at full speed.

"Sarrie! Are you alright?"

Quick, working as silently as possible, Mozze shoved her back into the deep shadows under the wolf's paw. He had little energy left, and he knew he had even less time left.

"Sarrie! Answer me!"

Mozze slinked into the opposite paw and lay quiet, waiting for his strength to flood back.

"She won't answer."

"And it's too quiet."

The guards approached the wolf, lit a torch, searched, and saw Sarrie bound up.

"What kind of bobotong is this?"

Mozze saw his chance. He summoned all the strength he had and attacked. He struck the nearest guard on the neck, shattering bones and the carotid artery. The man fell, choking in his own blood. Mozze snatched up his sword. Startled, the second guard reached for the horn hanging like a necklace on his chest, rather than for his sword. If it weren't for the lisis, Mozze might have killed him before the alarm sounded. He was a few heartbeats too slow. The man blew the pipe as the sword ripped his belly open. He fell, the little horn stuck on his mouth, filling with blood.

Mozze held his breath, hoping no one heard the short blast. But there came a reply, telling him that he had put his son's life in greater danger.

Mozze raced for the inner wall, keeping in the shadows, as a pandemonium of horns rocked the night. He used a creeping plant to scale the inner wall, which was only twenty feet high, jumped into the royal section, and hid in a shrub.

The pandemonium peaked. Two guards were dead. A deadly intruder lurked. Guards ran from here to there in total confusion. He tripped one who was running by, and broke his neck with a single blow. Quickly, he dragged the corpse into the shrub and waited. No one had seen it happen. He dressed up in the man's clothing. He folded his dreadlocks and hid them in a large scarf. Feeling safe in his disguise, he set out to help Jez.

He stayed near the shrub, to prevent other guards from searching it and finding the third dead guard, but he was still able to glean information from the jessis who ran to and fro. Some shouted orders at him. Others asked if he had orders for them. A great deal of time passed and still there was no sign of the intruder. Finally, Mozze let out a sigh. He smiled with himself, happy with what he had done. Maybe he had saved the king's life, and Jez had after all found a way out.

Just as he was beginning to bask in the comfort of this thought, the bell rang. It froze the night with gruesome peals that were loud enough to awake the entire city. It rang only to make important announcements. On such a night, it could only mean the king's death. Sure enough, the next set of guards who passed by verbally confirmed it. The king was dead. Slain in his sleep.

Another lisis attack sent Mozze to the ground. Fire burned his legs worse than ever. He took a sip of his medicine but the pain did not relent. He had to take two more sips before the torture ended.

Tears stung his eyes, the kind of tears that came when his father died. It was foolish of him to try to stop Jez, a naïve but very intelligent assassin, who had clearly thought of a way in and a way out. But Mozze's clumsiness had ruined the plan. How can Jez get out now? Surely, the commander who let him in won't help him out.

He had killed his son.

He waited for the news of the assassin's capture to reach him. He heard nothing. He learned that the assassin had sneaked into the palace dressed as a cobweb sweeper. When the alarm sounded, jessis closed the golden doors, unaware that the assassin was already inside. He slay eight guards before breaking into the royal bed chambers, where the king was fast asleep with his wife, and killed them both. He had then escaped through a window. The jessis now hunted for an assassin disguised as a cobweb sweeper.

Jez was more intelligent than Mozze had thought. He had an alternative way out. Mozze felt proud of him. But the death of the king and the thought of a rabbit-eared queen angered him.

Daybreak drew closer. The oleli bird, unaware of the tragedy, sang to lure the sun out of its bed. At another time, Mozze might have sung along. He won his wife's love by imitating the tiny songster ikinko, whose sweet voice causes flowers to bloom. But now he wanted to kill this oleli bird. To kill every musician. To destroy every song ever made and put an end to all singing. He lay in a stupor in the grass until the first rays of the sun touched the treetops and the bird fell quiet.

An idea struck him with such a force that he sat bolt upright. An idea that would stop that rabbit-eared creature from becoming queen. It would also give Jez a chance to escape, if Jez had not yet gotten out.

Even before the idea could solidify, Mozze pranced to the golden doors of the king's court, where a group of soldiers milled about in confusion. He removed the scarf hiding his dreadlocks and let his hair fall onto his back.

"I am the assassin," he said. "I have a message for Prince Manet."

#

After half a day in a windowless cell, they shackled him and took him to Prince Manet, who sat on the king's throne, though he was still a prince. His wife had a haughty face. She wore an elaborate crown that hid her rabbit ears. She sat on the queen's throne, at the right hand side of Prince Manet. Twelve guards stood in a row behind Mozze. They were in a large room. It had no furniture apart from the two thrones. The walls were bedecked with waxed heads of previous kings. A rug of leopard skin covered the entire floor. A thousand leopards must have died over hundreds of years to make the rug. Golden chandeliers hung overhead, holding candles that produced a sweet smell and too much soot. Artists used the soot to paint murals on the ceiling depicting the glory of the Bito Kingdom.

"Who are you?" the prince said.

"I'll speak in private," Mozze said. "It's about the inn at the foot of a mountain."

A long silence ensued. Prince Manet and his wife whispered to each other, obviously arguing. Eventually, Prince Manet stopped arguing and nodded to whatever she said. She then gave a command. Everybody except three guards withdrew from the room. Mozze remembered that three messengers had come to Hinko's inn. Were they these three guards?

"So talk," Prince Manet said. "Who are you?"

"You hired me."

"I did not."

"You wanted it done before the Elephant Festival. Any fool can decipher to whose advantage that is, since you married a rabbit-eared creature."

"We are people!" Manet's wife screeched. Her lips trembled in anger, her teeth clenched. "I'll kill you for this," she added.

"So what do you want?" Prince Manet asked.

"Help," Mozze said. "I have to get out."

"We can't help you," Manet's wife said. "If you can't get out–"

Mozze yelped in a feigned lisis attack, cutting her short. He fell down, crying, kicking his legs as though desperate to take off the boots.

"Lisis," the prince said. "The disease of the mountain people. We don't have the medicine to help you."

"I have my medicine!" Mozze cried, twitching, trying to reach for the vial.

"Let him help himself," the princess said.

One guard stepped to him. He had the keys to the shackles. He freed Mozze's hands. Mozze fished out the bottle and pretended to take a sip. He could not swallow for it would leave him weak. He needed strength for the next phase of his plan.

"I have to take off my shoes too," he cried.

The guard unshackled his feet. The moment the chains fell off, Mozze punched him in the throat, hard, shattering bones and tissue. The guard fell, gasping for air, chocking on his shattered larynx. Mozze snatched his sword and charged at the other two men. They were quick to meet his challenge, but they were no match for him. They fell within a few heartbeats.

The prince and his wife shouted for help, but they had locked out the other guards. They had nowhere to run. By the time the jessis forced their way in, they were both dead. Mozze had removed the crown from the woman's head and cut off her ears. Each was two feet long.

#

Prince Palla was crowned at the Elephant Festival. Six days later, Hinko visited Mozze, on the morning of the day he was to be executed.

"They refused to allow your family to see you," Hinko said.

On hearing that, even before Hinko told him what had happened, Mozze knew that Jez was alive. After killing King Amara, he had hidden in the ceiling of the kitchen. He had no hope of getting out until he overheard the cooks talking about the surrender of the assassin. He knew they had made a mistake, but this meant they were no longer searching for the man disguised as a cobweb cleaner. That night, he sneaked out of the ceiling and hid in a garbage cart. He did not know the identity of the captured assassin until he reached home. It changed his life.

"He asks for your forgiveness," Hinko said.

Mozze did not know what to say in reply. He was shackled to a chair. They were in the windowless cell. The air was damp and muggy. A long silence followed.

"When the time comes, listen hard. You will be blindfolded, but listen for his voice above the roar of the crowd."

They marched him out at noon. They made him lie face up on a large, flat stone. The sun kissed his face with hot lips. He longed for a cool breeze, for a cold shower. He wished the axe could fall before he heard his son's voice. He wished he was able to put his fingers into his ears and shut out the clamoring crowd, and his son. He could not. The voice crept into his head like a shy girl climbing into her lover's bed. Every other sound in the world faded away.

His son sang mpenzi moja. The lyrics wafted about like butterflies around flowers, blowing a cool breeze over him, making him smile. He was happy. Jez knew all the words to the song. How had he learnt them? How had he learnt to sing so beautifully in such a short time? He did not care for answers. Jez would make a very fine assassin, and an even finer musician. The pariah days were over for the family. Mozze started singing too, and his wife added her voice to the family choir. The axe fell, but the smile stayed frozen on Mozze's face.✷

Other Titles by Black Letter Media

- The Short Story is Dead, Long Live the Short Story
- Voices From My Clan - edited by Obinna Udenwe and Mukoma wa Ngugi
- My Holiday Shorts
- Poetry Potion print quarterly journal
- www.poetrypotion.com

www.blackletterm.com
find us on facebook.com/BlackLetterMedia

Other Titles by Dilman Dila

- The Terminal Move
- Cranes Crest at Sunset

www.dilmandila.com

Printed in Great Britain
by Amazon

10344110R00116